THE BABY DOCTORS

THE BABY DOCTORS

Alice Grey

CHIVERS

| British Library Cataloguing in Publication Data available |

This Large Print edition published by BBC Audiobooks Ltd, Bath, 2008.
Published by arrangement with the author.

U.K. Hardcover ISBN 978 1 408 41201 5
U.K. Softcover ISBN 978 1 408 41202 2

Printed and bound in Great Britain by
Antony Rowe, Chippenham, Wiltshire

CHAPTER ONE

'You look worried.'

Pippa reluctantly dragged her gaze from the Arrivals board at Heathrow Airport, and turned to the woman who had spoken, a plump lady with grey hair. She smiled. 'Do I?' The smile failed to hide the anxiety in her green eyes.

'You've done nothing but stare at the Arrivals board,' said her neighbour. 'Are you waiting for the New York flight?'

'No—Chile. Santiago. It was due in at two-fifteen. And they haven't yet put "delayed" on the board.'

'It's nearly half-past three,' said the woman. 'The New York flight is due any moment. My daughter is on it. She's been working in the States. She's a teacher. Special education.' She spoke proudly and Pippa smiled politely.

'I bet you're meeting someone special,' said the woman, with a coquettish glance. 'Your boyfriend? I can see you're not married because you don't wear a ring, and anyway, you're too young to be married.'

'I'm twenty-three,' said Pippa indignantly, and brushed back the vivid red curls from her forehead. 'And actually, it's my fiancé I'm meeting.'

Her fingers strayed to the fine silver chain

1

around her neck. She felt a little embarrassed as she said it. She'd told no one else. In fact, Neil hadn't really asked her to marry him. Not in so many words. No going down on bended knee and all that romantic nonsense. She couldn't imagine down-to-earth, bespectacled Neil doing anything like that.

It had just been an accepted thing that they would marry one day. After all, she'd known him for two years.

Nestling between her breasts on the silver chain was a ring. It had been his grandmother's, and he had given it to Pippa before setting off for Valparaiso, where he was working with premature babies. It was a beautiful ring, a large pearl surrounded by emeralds.

'To match your eyes,' he had said. It was heavy, set in antique silver, but much too small for Pippa's capable nurse's fingers.

'When I come home next time,' he had promised, 'I'll take it to the jewellers, get it enlarged.'

'I shan't be able to wear it on duty,' Pippa had reminded him. 'It's really beautiful, but you know it wouldn't be allowed. Not practical, either. All that scrubbing up for deliveries—well, it would probably get lost if I had to keep taking it off.'

'Well, of course, but it seems such a shame—'

'I'll wear it round my neck,' Pippa had said, compromising.

2

'And when I come home in June,' he had begun, holding her close to him, so she could hear his heart beating, and smell the musky odour of his aftershave. He hadn't finished the sentence, but she had known what he meant.

She could feel the coolness of the ring next to her skin. It kept reminding her.

'Fiancé?' The plump woman beamed. 'Oh, I love a nice wedding. I'm hoping my daughter will find a nice young man soon. She's a bit older than you. What does your fiancé do?'

'He's a children's doctor. He works with premature babies.'

'A baby doctor? Oh, that's lovely. That's the best sort of doctor to marry. He'll be so useful when you have your own.'

Pippa flushed. She had not thought that far ahead. In fact, she found it difficult to imagine herself and Neil with children. Or even getting married to Neil and going out to Chile . . .

Her green eyes fixed on the Arrivals board again. The New York flight had landed. What could have happened to the Santiago flight? She stood up.

'I'm going to find out,' she said.

The plump woman nodded. 'Yes. They'll know all about it,' she said soothingly.

Pippa didn't know who she meant by 'they', so she crossed the hall towards the Airport Information desk. Terminal Three, as always, was very busy. As usual, it smelled of disinfectant, coffee, and cheese and onion

3

crisps. Pippa threaded her way between the bustling people, avoiding small children and luggage trolleys. The girl at the desk was friendly and sympathetic, but she couldn't help.

'I'm sorry,' she told Pippa. 'If there is any news then the airline will have it. I expect it's VIASA.'

Pippa didn't know. 'I'm not sure.'

'Just over there.' She indicated a row of open cubicles, each printed with the name of a different airline.

'Thank you.' Pippa turned quickly, and collided heavily with a tall, male figure in a cream linen jacket, who had come up soundlessly behind her.

'Olivia!' Firm hands grasped her shoulders, preventing her from moving away. Bemused, she looked up into a lean, tanned face with a firm jaw, and the deepest blue eyes she had ever seen. Against her will, her pulses began to race, and her cheeks grew hot. He had addressed her as if he were thrilled to see her. And what had he called her? Olivia? But she had never seen him before in her life. She would never have forgotten those blue, blue eyes . . .

At the same moment of mutual realisation, he released her, and a frown appeared between his dark, well-shaped eyebrows.

'I'm sorry,' he said curtly. 'Thought you were someone else. Do you always go around

4

treading on people's toes?'

She stared at him for a moment, nonplussed. Quickly she recovered herself, and her green eyes flashed.

'Only metaphorically,' she retorted. Glancing down at his feet in their beige pigskin shoes, she added mischievously, 'I'm sorry if I've spoiled the shine.'

Tilting her chin, she turned and walked briskly away. She could feel his gaze boring into her back and her heart began to beat faster. She hadn't really trodden on his toes, she told herself as she crossed the hall. Halfway to her seat she instinctively looked up at the Arrivals board. Her hand went to her mouth. 'Flight VA710 from Santiago, via Caracas, cancelled. Refer to Airline.'

She hurried across to the VIASA Airline desk. People were already clustered there, arguing and gesticulating. The airline official, a pretty girl with chestnut hair, was trying to explain the situation.

'Why wasn't it on the news?' a burly man asked.

'You must realise—I'm sure you do—that earthquakes are frequent in Chile. Most of them are only small ones—'

Pippa held her breath. She hadn't thought of an earthquake, yet Neil had told her in his letters how they were happening all the time.

'Was this only a small one, then?' asked a swarthy woman in red. 'Was there much

5

damage?'

Pippa desperately wanted to ask, Was anyone killed? Was the hospital in Valparaiso affected? which was foolish, because how would they know?

'Five on the Richter Scale. Medium sized, I suppose, for Chile. There was some structural damage, I believe, but it was the older buildings that suffered. They had to inspect the runways before they could allow any flights in or out, and that takes time. I'm very sorry.'

There was a moment's silence. They all started to talk at once. The girl lifted her hand.

'I can assure you it is only a temporary problem. The next flight is expected here tomorrow, at around 1700 hours. If you ring here in the morning we can tell you definitely.'

Most of the crowd began to disperse, grumbling among themselves. Pippa felt she'd just reached the bottom of a roller-coaster. She had been looking forward to today. And now he wasn't going to arrive. Yet, in a strange way, she was relieved. And she didn't know why. She sank down into a seat next to the plump woman, who glanced curiously at her.

'Delayed?' she asked brightly.

'Cancelled. The next flight's tomorrow. An earth-quake.' She spoke tersely, unsure of her feelings.

'Oh, dear. That is a shame. Have you come far?'

'Basingstoke. It isn't that—it's just that—

well, I was all keyed up for today—after six months . . .' Tears of frustration were threatening. She bit her lip and fiddled with her bag.

'Why don't you go and get a cup of coffee? Do you good,' the plump woman suggested. 'Oh—there's Alison! Yoo-hoo!' She hurried across the hall to meet a short, brown-haired girl with owlish glasses. They hugged and kissed tearfully, which made Pippa feel worse. She turned away from the emotional scene, trying to push back the thought that by now she should have been driving back to Hampshire with Neil beside her. But she couldn't help thinking—Suppose he never came back? Suppose the earthquake had damaged the hospital—or the house where he lived?

She hurried into the café and ordered a cup of coffee. She knew she was indulging her vivid imagination, but she could just see herself answering the phone, hearing a voice say, 'He was off duty, it was an old house, it just collapsed, he didn't stand a chance.' She could see Neil's elderly parents' grief-stricken faces, hear their heartbroken words

'Excuse me, is it possible to get to the counter?' She spun on her heel, and her full cup of coffee rattled in the saucer, spilling over the edge and splashing.

'Oh! Sorry!'

'You again!' He dabbed angrily at the beige

7

spots which had appeared on the front of his cream jacket. Pippa stared in dismay.

'Not content with bruising my inoffensive toes, you now attempt to scald me with boiling coffee!' he berated her, his deep voice harsh with annoyance.

'But it—'

'You seem determined to injure me in some way. I don't know what I've done to deserve it. I've never seen you before in my life!'

He reached the counter and ordered two coffees and a glass of milk.

'Oh!' Pippa was desperately trying to find suitable words of protest. He turned and looked at her, and a shock seemed to run through her body.

'You still here?'

Pippa was aware of the café staff watching with amusement. One of them, a fat girl with spots, was staring at him, goggle-eyed.

It's only his good looks, Pippa said angrily to herself. Handsome is as handsome does. One of her mother's favourite sayings when she referred to Pippa's father.

The tall man took the drinks to a table, ignoring Pippa. She had missed her opportunity now of retaliation, so she squeezed into a seat in a corner and tried not to look at him. He really was so attractive, those deep blue eyes when he was angry . . .

He had joined a young, dark-haired woman in a print dress. And parked between them was

8

a child in a wheelchair, a pale, blonde girl whose twisting features and writhing limbs betrayed her severe handicap. The man leaned towards the woman to hear what she was saying, his expression attentive. Then he laughed.

He looks so much nicer when he smiles, thought Pippa. He's got lovely white teeth. She watched wistfully as he carefully held the glass of milk to the little girl's mouth, wiping gently with a tissue when some of it trickled down her chin.

Lucky child, she thought. Then brought herself up sharply. Lucky? With cerebral palsy? Whatever was she thinking?

She drained her cup. There was nothing to keep her here. Still she hesitated. To leave she had to pass their table, and she'd had enough of his unfair comments for one day. Perhaps she should wait until they'd gone. But no—that would be cowardly. And she had done nothing to be ashamed of. The coffee stains were only just visible from where she sat. And that had been his own fault. He'd startled her, twice he'd come up behind her and made her jump. Almost as though he'd done it on purpose. And then he'd had the nerve to pretend he'd only just noticed her, when her vivid red hair must have been easily visible from the door. She got up and picked up her bag.

Holding her pale blue jacket close to her

9

body, she manoeuvred her way between the tables to reach the door. She didn't want him to see her. Part of her didn't, anyway. The lightweight fabric of the jacket hugged her figure, emphasising her firm breasts and her trim waist and hips. The man was deep in conversation with his wife, and Pippa held her breath as she passed. Then, just as she eased herself past the handles of the folding wheelchair, two boisterous youths came pushing behind her, upsetting her precarious balance. She grabbed at the wheelchair to stop herself falling—and a strong hand shot out and covered hers.

'Good heavens, woman, are you accident-prone?'

There was a brief, awful moment when everyone seemed to stop talking. The youths had gone, unaware of the consequences of their uncouth behaviour. Pippa flushed with anger and mortification. Yet, at the same time she was only too conscious of the warmth and strength in the hand on hers.

'Don't shout at me like that!' she cried furiously, wrenching her hand away. Her green eyes were bright with unshed tears. As if things weren't bad enough already, with Neil not turning up, but this—this awful man could do nothing but abuse her, for things that weren't her fault. The unfairness of it all made her mouth tremble.

'Please—Julian,' the dark-haired woman

10

said soothingly, 'it wasn't her fault. Those youths pushed her. Didn't you see it?'

'I only saw she almost tipped Amy on to the floor,' he said grimly.

'But she couldn't help it—'

Pippa was trying to control herself. She was still angry, but confused because she could still feel the pressure of his hand on hers. She tried to massage it away.

'All right,' said Julian, in a tight voice, and, when he wasn't shouting at her, Pippa thought what a nice voice he had. Like dark brown velvet.

'All right, Stella, she didn't mean to do it, but the fact remains she's obviously accident-prone, and it would please me greatly if she'd remove herself at least twenty feet from here, preferably more. Dammit, she's a red-head! Isn't that enough?'

Pippa drew herself up to her full five feet five inches. It was difficult to remain in control when those deep blue eyes were watching her. She tilted her chin defiantly.

'I'd be only too pleased to remove myself away from you,' she said in a tight voice. 'I've never met such an objectionable man in my life! I don't know what makes you think you have the right to talk to people in this way, but I pity your poor wife!'

With a glance at Stella, she swung away from the table and out through the door. Once out of sight of the café's occupants, she

11

paused, breathing hard. What an obnoxious man! He'd quite ruined her day. No, that wasn't quite true. It had been ruined before she'd met him, but he hadn't done anything to improve it.

She couldn't see the plump woman and her daughter anywhere, so she hoisted her bag on her shoulder and went out to the car park, where her ancient blue Escort was waiting.

She really must calm down, she told herself, as she got in and started the engine. As if it mattered what he thought of her, or she of him. She'd never see him again.

*   *   *

Soon she was on the M25 and heading for the junction with the M3, to Basingstoke and Winchester. On the rear seat of her car sat a bulging supermarket carrier bag, with prawns and chicken, rice and peppers, grapefruit, expensive fresh strawberries and double cream. Well, she wouldn't use it now. Unless Lucy wanted to help her eat it. But wasn't she going to a party tonight?

Pippa had intended it to be such a special evening. Just Neil and herself, dining on paella and drinking wine by candlelight—and she'd remembered the candles—then listening to soft music while he talked about his work in Valparaiso. Neil had told her very little about the hospital in his letters, except to say it was

12

new, had five hundred beds, and was on the coast. The premature baby unit was one of the best in South America, he'd told her. He expected to get some good experience, especially with the high birth-rate and infant mortality. They needed more midwives, he had tactfully added. Pippa had thought she wanted to go. Now she was not so sure, but she didn't know what had changed her mind.

She left the junction and started down the wide motorway. Her car was due for its annual MOT soon; she wasn't sure it would pass. It was starting to make funny little noises. She hoped they weren't serious. She really needed a new car. She'd seen a nice Astra at a dealer's in Basingstoke, a red one. Only two thousand pounds and a B registration! But, on a pupil midwife's salary, how could she possibly afford it? Of course she wouldn't always be a pupil. In a few weeks she'd be taking her finals, and she'd get a salary rise when she became a staff midwife. That was, if she stayed here, and didn't go to Chile, and didn't marry Neil.

She sighed. She'd really set her heart on the red Astra. The old blue Escort had fortunately seen her through her community experience, three months delivering babies in their own homes. She'd managed to get her quota quite easily, and even a few more. Until recently the trend had been for all babies to be born in hospital, but now it was changing, and more mothers were demanding to have their babies

13

at home, among family, away from all the modern technology, induced labours, epidurals, and often unnecessary Caesareans.

She yawned. She'd had a busy, if rather wasted, day. It was no fun spending your only day off hanging around an airport lounge. Her foot relaxed slightly on the accelerator, and a cream-coloured Rover began to overtake her. She glanced across—and her heart missed a beat. Her hands slipped damply on the steering wheel and the car veered fractionally to the left. Fortunately, her reflexes were quick and she soon regained full concentration. Inwardly, her heart was thudding, and she could hardly breathe. She certainly hadn't expected to see *him* on this road!

His wife—Stella?—had been looking straight ahead, and the child, Amy, appeared to be asleep, strapped in the rear seat. But their presence had barely registered on Pippa's consciousness. Her gaze had focused on that lean profile with the strong jaw, and dark wavy hair falling over his brow. It all happened in a second. Even as she realised who it was, the car was almost out of sight on the fast lane.

Pippa cursed under her breath. She was quite stupid, letting a perfect stranger, and particularly one as ob-noxious as he was, to upset her emotional equilibrium. She was engaged to Neil, who was kind, gentle and calm, and who loved her. He wasn't especially nice-looking, but that didn't matter. Other

14

virtues were more important. But six months was a long time, and it was hard to remember how he'd looked the last time she'd seen him, just after Christmas at Heathrow. He had worn a sheepskin jacket, and black cords. She remembered that. She remembered his broad smile that made his eyes crinkle up. He had a dimple. And his yellow hair flopped about like a child's. She tried to remember his clear grey eyes behind the gold-rimmed spectacles, but all she could see was a pair of deep, deep blue ones, long-lashed, and an angry frown between dark brown eyebrows.

Damn him! He'd certainly got under her skin. She'd probably been dreaming—she hadn't seen him in that cream Rover at all, just someone like him. She reached the outskirts of Basingstoke with relief. Within a short time she had parked her car outside the hospital residence, grabbed her handbag and the plastic carrier of groceries, and was going up in the lift to the second floor. She felt incredibly weary and depressed.

*   *   *

'Cancelled?' Lucy Waters kicked off her shoes and flung herself into an armchair.

'A slight earthquake.' Pippa felt she couldn't elaborate; she was feeling too emotional.

'A what? An earthquake?' There was no denying Lucy the facts.

15

'Not a big one. He's probably coming tomorrow. I have to ring in the morning to find out. And that's the snag, Lucy. He'll expect me to be there. And I've got a split shift. I can't possibly get there for five o'clock! Or six, or seven, or eight!'

She took the carrier bag crossly into the kitchen, and dumped it on the table.

'And there's all this food! It's going to be wasted.'

'What have you got?' Lucy had come up behind her in her stockinged feet, and now peered at the packages and paper bags. 'Oo—prawns, strawberries, cream! And a bottle of wine!'

'I was going to make a paella. Neil loves paella. It was going to be something special. And I can't do it tomorrow night, I'm working. And you're going out tonight—'

'It will keep, Pippa. Put it in the fridge. And—hey—an idea—why don't I do it? I can cook, you know.'

'I know, but I'm working. You do mean tomorrow?'

'I've got a half-day.' She flushed. 'Actually, I meant I could cook it for Neil. And I could meet him at the airport, if you like.' She spoke casually.

'Lucy, I can't let you do that. It's kind of you to offer, but it's your half-day . . .' She put the prawns and chicken in the fridge.

'I don't mind. Honest.' Lucy went over to

16

the window and looked out. 'I'm not doing anything else.'

'Well, it would certainly solve my problem.'

'That's settled then. And I'll save you some paella, too, if you like.'

'It doesn't matter. There's only enough for two. You eat it. I'd like you to have it.'

Lucy didn't answer straight away. Her fingers clenched the edge of the window-sill. She turned to look at Pippa, her round cheeks still pink.

'Thanks, Pippa. At least let me pay for it.'

'For heaven's sake, Lucy! It's for Neil, isn't it? I can't let you pay for it. He's my fiancé, after all.'

She could have bitten out her tongue. She reddened. Lucy's round blue eyes widened.

'You're engaged? Since when?'

'Lucy—it's not really official—I shouldn't have said anything. Please don't tell anyone.'

'Don't? Why not?'

Pippa bit her lip. Why not indeed? Neil wouldn't mind. And all their friends assumed they'd marry eventually. Why not tell them now? What was holding her back? She swallowed.

'I'd rather wait until Neil gets back,' she said, trying to sound positive. 'I want to choose the right moment.' Lucy gave her a shrewd look. Pippa played with a packet of rice. 'You see, we haven't told the parents yet. They should be the first to know. Don't you agree,

17

Lucy?'

Lucy sat down at the table. Her long ash-blonde hair was coming loose from its moorings.

'Yes, Pippa, they should. I won't say a word. But I can understand how anxious you are to get it all arranged. The wedding, I mean. Who wouldn't be, with someone like Neil?' She got up again. 'Well, I'd better get ready for the party. I can't decide what to wear. Something to make me look slimmer, in case I meet someone nice!'

She left the kitchen, and Pippa could hear her moving about in her room. She'd got it wrong, of course, about her and Neil. It was Neil who was rushing the wedding. All those hints. And the ring. But would he ever ask her properly? Suddenly, she felt she needed more time to think.

In her room, Lucy was muttering to herself. Pippa went into the corridor. Something about Lucy was bothering her. What was it?

'Mike Badger's leaving party, is it?' she called out. There was a mumbled reply. Through Lucy's half-open door she could see her flatmate pulling off her white uniform dress, tossing her dark blue staff midwife's belt over a chair. On the bed lay three dresses in different colours.

Pippa remembered. When she'd accidentally announced her engagement, Lucy hadn't congratulated her. Or had she been too disconcerted to notice?

'I'd better have a shower,' said Lucy, grabbing her brown woollen dressing gown. 'Need the bathroom?'

'I've got all evening,' said Pippa. 'I'm not doing anything.'

'Oh, Pippa, I'm so sorry!' Lucy hugged her. 'You must be feeling awful. And here am I, fussing about what dress to wear.'

'Don't worry about me,' Pippa reassured her. 'Go and enjoy yourself. Wear that one, with the black skirt and lilac top. It suits you.'

'Does it? I'd like to create a good impression at my first doctor's leaving party.'

'Well, now you're a staff midwife you'll be invited to them all.'

'You won't have long to wait, Pippa. A few weeks. That's if you stay on—oh, of course, I don't suppose you will. Neil will—'

'He wants me to go out to Chile with him. They need midwives.'

'Oh, what an opportunity! If someone asked me I'd jump at it!' She looked hard at Pippa. 'You are going, of course?'

Pippa shrugged her shoulders. 'Well, if I'm married to Neil—'

'Yes, you'd have to, wouldn't you? Lucky you!'

'I'm not sure—'

'You're so lucky to have someone like Neil. He deserves the best, don't you agree?'

'Oh, yes, he's a wonderful person—'

'He deserves someone who'll stand by him, support him—and I know you do, Pippa. I know how much you love him. He's lucky to have someone like you.'

Flushed, her eyes bright, she grabbed her towel and disappeared into the bathroom.

Oh, God! thought Pippa.

CHAPTER TWO

The alarm clock woke Pippa at seven o'clock next morning. She sat up and yawned, before slipping into her green cotton dressing gown and fluffy mules, and padding out to the kitchen. She had slept fitfully, seemed to have done nothing but dream about earthquakes and Neil. Only he hadn't really looked like Neil—his face seemed to be made of plaster, and as he bent to kiss her it began to crack and crumble. Someone said it was only a small earthquake for Chile, and then his eyes, all that was left, were deep blue, and he was in a wheelchair, running away out of control, and he was shouting back at her, 'Accident-prone! Accident-prone!'

She'd woken up in a sweat, and had lain there for quite a while, feeling disturbed and anxious. This morning she didn't feel much better. She had to ring Heathrow quite early. It would have to be in her coffee break.

She switched on the kettle and tipped some muesli into a dish. They were a bit low on milk. Perhaps Lucy would get some when she went to meet Neil.

Water was running in the bathroom. Lucy was singing 'Some Enchanted Evening'. Pippa found herself humming. Her flatmate must have had a good time at the party. Perhaps she'd met someone nice. Perhaps she'd even fallen in love! Of course, the new senior registrar would probably have been there, the one who was replacing Mike Badger. Pippa knew Lucy had a soft spot for Mike, but it was no use her hoping for anything more. He was already married, and had a three-year-old daughter whom everyone adored. The new registrar could quite easily be single. And if he were, even if he were fat and balding with warts on his nose and a glass eye, there'd be some nurses who'd chase after him.

Pippa thought smugly, I can afford to be tolerant. I don't need to look at the new doctors in a predatory way. I can take them or leave them. Lucy came into the kitchen, looking all damp and pink. Her long fair hair hung around her shoulders, making her appear about sixteen, instead of twenty-six. She sat at the table and poured herself orange juice.

'Nice party?' asked Pippa, chewing muesli.

'I was going to tell you all about it last night,' said Lucy. 'But you were asleep.'

'All that travelling, I suppose. I could hardly

keep my eyes open. I didn't even hear you come in. Was it very late?'

'About twelve.' She put a slice of bread in the toaster.

'Well, go on! Tell me all about it. Who was there? Mike, of course.'

'Of course. And the usual crowd, the sisters, a couple of consultants, old Big-Ears—' Pippa grinned at the nickname of one of the senior doctors, a pompous elderly man with sticking-out ears '—and a few medical students. The usual crowd.' She spoke casually, kept her glance averted.

'Anyone special?'

'No—oh, you mean the new registrar. Yes, he was there, but he didn't stay long.' She drained her glass and got up. 'Coffee?'

'Oh—yes, please.'

Lucy moved about the table, putting coffee into mugs, looking at the carton of milk and shaking it.

'Not much milk.'

'No. What is he like?'

'All right, I suppose. Tall. I only spoke to him once. Annette Foster appropriated him most of the time. Made a fuss of him. You know what she's like.'

'Don't we all?' said Pippa. Annette Foster was a junior sister on the Delivery Suite where Pippa was at present working. And, thinking back to her earlier reflection that some nurses would set their cap at the most unlikely male

22

doctors, Pippa realised that Annette Foster certainly fitted the bill. Divorced after a short early marriage, childless and now well over thirty, she had an air of desperation about her. It was as if seeing all those mothers and their babies reminded her how time was flying. Yes, it was only to be expected she'd make a bee-line for the new registrar. And she was quite attractive, with raven black hair and big brown eyes.

Surprising, thought Pippa, that she hadn't been snapped up before now. Could it be she made her predatory intentions too obvious?

The coffee was hot. Pippa added the last of the milk. Lucy spread marmalade on her toast.

'What's his name?' asked Pippa, although she'd know soon enough. She'd probably meet him today on the Delivery Suite. She smiled to herself. Supposing he was fat and balding, with warts on his nose and a glass eye . . . ?

'Not sure,' said Lucy. 'Rees or Reed. Didn't quite catch it. It was a noisy party. Reed, I think. Not sure about his first name. Could have been George or Joe or Adrian. Not sure. He didn't stay long. Annette got the sulks.'

She crammed the last bit of toast into her mouth and got up.

'Come on, Pippa. You can't sit there dreaming about the new senior registrar. We're on duty in fifteen minutes. And, besides, you're already engaged.'

'Beast!' called Pippa after her, as she went

23

down to her room. 'And anyway, I wasn't dreaming about him. I don't expect he's my type at all.'

'I suppose not,' said Lucy, her voice muffled as she struggled into her white dress. 'He's not a bit like Neil.'

For a moment, Pippa had to force herself to remember what Neil looked like. Deep blue eyes . . . No, no, no . . .

Minutes later, in clean uniform dresses, they walked down the long, airy corridor from the Staff Residence to the hospital.

Kingslake Maternity Hospital was fairly new, about ten years old, built to serve the growing population of Basingstoke, after an antiquated hospital—much loved by the town's residents—had been pulled down to make way for an improved ring road. Kingslake had been built on the same site as a large general hospital, and some of the facilities were shared, such as the physiotherapy school and the college of radiotherapy. Nurses completing their general training often decided to follow it with midwifery training at Kingslake. Pippa had done this, although Lucy had come from a large London hospital.

The two girls had hit it off from the start, even though Lucy was four months ahead of Pippa. Yet, although Pippa had always been frank and honest with Lucy, she sometimes had the feeling that Lucy was holding back. Sometimes she felt she hardly knew her. She

24

often wondered why Lucy had left London. She'd mentioned lots of her friends who were still there, and she sometimes went to see them. Pippa felt sure it was a love-affair gone wrong. She wouldn't pry. Lucy might tell her one day. That was, if Pippa was still around, and not in Chile . . .

They reached the main reception hall, carpeted in dark blue, with small white tables and dark blue and white chairs.

'I'll tell you at lunchtime whether Neil's arriving at five,' Pippa promised, as she turned towards the corridor leading to the Delivery Suite.

'Oh—yes.' Lucy went a bit pink and hurried into a lift before the doors closed.

The hospital was a hive of activity, even at eight o'clock. Babies arrived when they felt like it—they didn't conform to office hours, nine to five! Humming 'Some Enchanted Evening'—it was one of those tunes that kept on and on, you couldn't get rid of it—Pippa hurried along to the Delivery Suite. After hanging her cloak on a peg in the cloakroom, she went along to Sister's office, where the report was given at the beginning of every shift. About eight pupil midwives, and a couple of staff midwives, were already seated there, notepads on their knees. Pippa joined them, just as Night Sister put down the phone and turned to face them.

'You're in for a busy day,' she began, and

25

the girl next to Pippa gave a mock groan. Night Sister glanced at her, and proceeded to read from the Kardex. There had been seven admissions during the night, two of them in the past half-hour. These were still in the admission suite, where recordings were done, showers given—if time!—before being transferred to either a labour-room or a delivery-room.

Most of the remaining patients seemed to be quite straightforward, and Pippa started to relax. The day-shift nurses began to fidget.

'Mrs Diane Emery is twenty-three,' said Night Sister. 'Primip.' Pippa wrote down—'preg one'. 'She attended clinic three days ago, and her blood-pressure was slightly raised. In view of this she was given an earlier appointment, for one week instead of two. She is thirty-one weeks pregnant.'

Pippa began to wonder what was coming. A typical case of toxaemia? Or something worse? She tensed, her pen over the paper.

'She complained of headache yesterday, to a neighbour, and indigestion.' Pippa held her breath. She'd been reading about this only the other day. She knew what was coming.

'Mr Emery didn't arrive home until seven o'clock, when he found her unconscious on the kitchen floor. While he waited for the ambulance, she suffered an eclamptic fit. It was probably her second.'

The nurses scribbled madly. Fulminating

eclampsia was a rare condition. Eclampsia usually took weeks to reach this level of severity.

'Is the baby—' began one of them.

'Of course it is at great risk,' said Night Sister. 'But it seems to be holding its own at the moment. Mrs Emery is under deep sedation. There is the possibility of Caesarean section eventually, but we think it is likely she is already in labour. But we daren't disturb her to find out which stage she's at. It might precipitate another fit.'

The nurses closed their notebooks and looked at each other, wondering who would have the responsibility of looking after such a complicated case. Sister Brayford, the Day Sister, smiled and allocated them their patients. Admission-room, labour-rooms, Delivery-Room Eight, where a teenager was almost in the second stage.

Soon only Pippa and a junior called Gillian Dale were left. And then they knew. The only patient left was Diane Emery. Sister smiled at them.

'Nurse Garland. Nurse Dale. You are to special Mrs Emery until she delivers. On no account is she to be left alone for one second. Is that clear? There are regular observations to be made, but Staff Midwife Jones will give you the details when you arrive. She is in Delivery-Room Three. The room is to be kept dim at all times. Off you go.'

Pippa's palms were clammy. She put her pen in her pocket and followed Gillian along the short corridor to the delivery-rooms. At Room Three they paused and looked at each other.

'Gosh,' said Gillian. 'Eclampsia. I've never seen it before.' Pippa smiled encouragingly. It was easy to think of the junior pupils as new to the hospital environment when in actual fact most pupil midwives were already registered nurses, quite capable of taking care of any emergency. Still, eclampsia was a frightening experience, where both mother's and child's lives were at risk. Pippa found she couldn't admit to Gillian she'd never met one, either.

'We'll manage,' she said, and pushed open the door. The pale green blinds were drawn over the windows, and a low-wattage light shone over the bed and on the charts laid out on the side cupboards.

'Thought you were never coming,' said Staff Midwife Jones in a low voice. 'Here, put these on.' She handed them paper hats and masks, and polythene aprons.

The girl on the delivery table was very still, and only her rather noisy breathing could be heard. Drips ran into her hands which lay calmly on top of the single cotton sheet. It was hot in the room.

'How is she?' asked Pippa.

'Fairly stable. Blood pressure still variable. Foetal heart satisfactory. That drip is

28

Puroverine for her blood-pressure, that one is lytic cocktail, Largactil, pethidine, you know.'

After a few more instructions, the night nurses left, pulling off their paper hats. Pippa and Gillian took over. For the next hour they worked quietly in the darkened delivery-room, taking recordings, checking the drips and the renal output.

'Her face is a bit puffy,' Gillian remarked. 'I bet she's usually quite pretty.' She gently pushed a lock of dark auburn hair off the girl's damp forehead.

Pippa smiled, then frowned, and checked the blood-pressure again. It shouldn't have gone that high in fifteen minutes—As Pippa's eyes met Gillian's over the bed, Diane groaned and moved restlessly. Pippa grabbed the rubber wedge from the tray and pushed it between Diane's teeth, just as the girl arched her back and her face went blue.

Gillian pressed the emergency button, and as the girl jerked convulsively she had to exert all her strength to prevent her falling from the table.

Once she was sure that the wedge was safely keeping Diane's jaws apart, Pippa quickly turned on the oxygen and placed the mask over the girl's face. So busy were they, performing the emergency procedures, that she was only vaguely aware of doors opening and closing, and soft running feet. Trolleys were wheeled across the floor, commands were quietly given. Hands injected Valium into one of the drips, and within seconds the convulsions began to lessen. Pippa watched as Diane's contorted face gradually relaxed. Only then did she turn to see what the others were doing.

Diane's legs had been put into lithotomy stirrups, and the lower part of her body was draped in green towels.

'Just as I thought,' said the doctor at the foot of the table, and he straightened up from his examination. His voice was deep but soft. Pippa felt her heart speed up. His head was still bent. She couldn't see his face, only a lock of dark hair straying from under his paper hat. 'She's in the second stage,' he said, looking up, and for a moment his deep blue eyes rested on Pippa. But only for a second.

'I'll need low forceps, Sister,' he said. 'How's the foetal heart?'

He was looking at her again. For a brief moment she couldn't move. Her heart was out of control, and she couldn't breathe. She cursed herself for falling under his spell yet again, and listened carefully to the baby's heartbeat.

'Slowing,' she said, and her voice seemed breathy and weak.

'What's that?' he demanded, in that familiar brusque tone. She could still remember his words of reprimand, given only yesterday.

'What exactly do you mean, Nurse? Be

explicit, please. Lives are at stake.'

She swallowed. It was fortunate he couldn't see how pink she was.

'It was one-fifty-five. It's now one-twenty-five.'

'No time to lose. Where are those damned forceps?'

'Here, Dr Reed.' Sister slipped the steel instruments from their sterile wrapping on to the waiting trolley. The new senior registrar checked the instruments and began to swab. Gillian was giving Diane oxygen. Pippa checked the foetal heart again. One-fifteen.

Dr Reed gently but skilfully inserted the shiny forceps. Over by the resuscitator, the paediatrician waited. Sister stood at Dr Reed's shoulder, her large brown eyes watching every move, occasionally giving him an adoring glance. Annette Foster. Pippa hadn't realised she was on duty. She hadn't been there for report.

'Foetal heart one hundred,' said Pippa, in a clear voice. It seemed to echo in the tense, quiet room.

'It's got a chance then,' murmured Dr Reed, and he slowly, expertly, began to draw out the tiny baby. The head was born. Its face was blue. Quickly, the body was delivered. A boy. But how tiny he was! His body was reddish mauve and shiny, his back covered with a dark downy fluff. Like a skinned rabbit, thought Pippa, and she willed him to breathe. He was

31

very still, his eyes closed.

The cord was cut, and the paediatrician transferred him to the resuscitation table. The room was too quiet, full of expectancy, waiting. Pippa was tense. She clenched her fists. Please, God, make him cry! she prayed silently. There were tears in Gillian's eyes. 'Blood-pressure falling,' she said quietly.

Pippa waited for Dr Reed's curt admonishment to be more explicit. Over at the table, the baby had been incubated, and was receiving oxygen. It looked pinker, thought Pippa. Oh, please . . .

Suddenly, a soft mewing broke the silence. Glances met. Pippa held her breath. It came again, a little louder, a little stronger. Her gaze met Dr Reed's, and those deep blue eyes made her heart pound anew. Then he looked away.

'Can you be more explicit, Nurse?' he asked Gillian, but his voice was less harsh.

'One-sixty over ninety-five,' said Gillian, a blush almost reaching her paper cap. So I'm not alone, thought Pippa. Everyone seems to have fallen under his spell.

It was all over now. Anti-climax. Everyone began to talk in low voices. The baby was hurried in an incubator down to the Special Care Baby Unit. SCBU, the nurses called it. Dr Reed stood up and pulled off his gloves. He pushed away the untidy trolley, with its used swabs, needles, forceps. Annette Foster pulled down her mask and looked up at him.

'You did a good job there, Julian,' she said quietly. Dr Reed frowned. He didn't answer for a moment, and moved away from the table. 'I'll write up the notes.' Sister Foster's smile faded slightly. She pulled off her paper hat and crumpled it in her hand. 'I shall be in the office should you need me,' she said. He nodded, and she left the room, smoothing her dress over her trim hips.

Diane was still sleeping. Gillian wheeled away the trolley and began to clear it in the utility room. Pippa was acutely aware of the registrar's nearness as he checked Diane's pulse. Flustered, she crossed to the cupboards, knocking a ballpoint pen to the floor. As she bent to pick it up a shadow fell across her.

'So it is you.'

Her heart thudding, she straightened up. He reached out and gently pulled down her mask. His deep blue eyes seemed to scrutinise her, and a thrill ran through her. Then she was angry with herself for letting him have this effect on her. No way could she let him know how she felt. Her eyes widened.

'I beg your pardon?'

'You were at the airport. I thought I recognised that red hair, even though not much of it is showing.' Again he reached out, and pulled off the paper hat which covered her damp red curls.

'Oh—the airport—oh yes, I remember now. You must be that insufferable man who did nothing but yell at me.'

She turned to the charts and began to write. Her hand was shaking. He was even smiling at her caustic remarks! She couldn't help noticing his mouth turned up naturally at the corners. A mouth made for laughter. And kissing? A guilty flush crept over her cheeks. Thank goodness he didn't know what she was thinking.

She could feel those lapis lazuli eyes on her, and she desperately wanted to look into them, to sink into those deep blue depths . . .

'I realised it was you when you knocked the pen to the floor,' he said softly, with a crooked smile. At once she recalled her humiliation at the airport, in front of his wife and daughter. She tightened her lips. It was so stupid to feel like this about a married man. And she was sort of engaged to Neil. The thought disturbed her. She closed the file.

'Does Mrs Emery have to stay here?' she asked lightly. He moved away, back to the table.

'If her blood-pressure hasn't risen she can go up to Ward Six to be specialled. Perhaps you'd check it?'

Pippa connected the cuff to the machine, aware that he was standing very close, almost touching her. She laid her fingers on the girl's pulse.

'Is it as rapid as yours?' asked Dr Reed quietly. Pippa flushed with annoyance. He was

34

insufferable! The conceit of him, to imagine her pulse was rapid because he was standing close to her. What made it worse, he was always so damned right! She took Diane's blood-pressure quickly, and rolled up the cuff.

'One-fifty-five over ninety-five.'

'Systolic fallen slightly. I think she can go upstairs quite soon. I'll get it arranged. Oh— check temperature and bleeding. I'll do the notes.' Pippa took a deep breath. He didn't have to remind her to do what was routine. Behind them the door opened.

'Excuse me, Dr Reed—' They turned, and Annette Foster's eyes narrowed. Julian Reed moved away from the table.

'Did you want me, Sister?' he asked.

'If you've finished here,' said Annette sweetly, 'I'll make some tea. And I've managed to rescue a few chocolate biscuits. Specially for you.' She darted a superior glance at Pippa.

'Not for me, thank you,' said Dr Reed. 'I never eat between meals.'

'Oh.' Sister Foster looked across at Pippa, filling in the blood-pressure chart. 'Don't be long finishing up in here, Nurse Garland,' she said sharply. 'We're going to need this room soon.' She took Julian's arm. 'That's one of the reasons I came, Julian. I've a feeling Mrs Linney may be in deep transverse arrest.'

'Why didn't you tell me that first?' he said sharply. 'I'll come straight away.' He hurried from the room, and Sister Foster ran after him, protesting.

Pippa looked across at Diane, who was stirring. She wiped the girl's face with a damp flannel. Diane opened her eyes.

'You're all right,' said Pippa, gently. 'It's all over.' Behind her Gillian wheeled in a clean trolley, ready for the next delivery.

'Diane's going up to Ward Six,' said Pippa, inserting a thermometer under Diane's armpit. 'As soon as they come for her.'

Diane was gazing at them in a bemused fashion. 'Please—tell me what happened—' her eyes seemed to notice for the first time her flat abdomen, and the tubing running into her veins '—the baby—what happened to the baby?' She struggled to sit up, and Pippa gently urged her down again, placing a pillow under her head.

'You were taken ill. Your blood-pressure went up, and you lost consciousness. And you went into labour.'

'But the baby wasn't due—not for nine weeks—'

'I know. He was rather small, but you're not to worry. He's being looked after in the Special Unit.'

'A boy,' said Diane softly. 'Carl wanted a boy.' She looked anxiously around. 'Where is Carl? Does he know? What time is it?'

Pippa glanced at the clock. 'Ten-fifteen.'

'At night? Oh, my God—'

'No. Morning. Please don't worry, Diane, it

36

isn't good for you. Your husband does know. He brought you to the hospital yesterday evening.'

'I remember peeling potatoes—the radio was on—music—I had a dreadful headache—and a violent pain in my side—'

Pippa nodded. She'd been very lucky. The door opened and Lucy came in.

'Is this Mrs Emery? Is she ready?'

'Yes—oh, no—he went without writing up the notes.'

'Will you bring her up then? As soon as they're done? I can't take her without the notes.'

'I'll take them to him now. Gillian, will you stay here until I get back?'

As she walked down the corridor with Lucy, it crossed Pippa's mind that she could have sent Gillian to get the notes written up. She didn't need to see that critical Dr Reed herself. And, against her will, her pulses began to race.

'Have you rung Heathrow yet?' asked Lucy.

'Haven't even been to coffee yet. I'll see you at lunch, I expect.' They reached the doctors' office. The door was ajar. Low voices could be heard.

'What's he like—the new registrar?' asked Lucy quietly, glancing at the door. Pippa felt her face grow warm.

'I suppose he's all right. But a bit too critical for my liking.' Lucy pulled a face, just as the door opened wide and a young fair-haired man came into the corridor. Behind him, Dr Reed laid a fatherly hand on his shoulder.

'If you wait a few moments, Mr Emery, you can go up to the ward with her.'

'Thank you, Doctor, for all you've done.' He shook the registrar's hand enthusiastically. Lucy disappeared down the corridor, and only then did Dr Reed seem to be aware of Pippa's presence. She held out the notes.

'Mrs Emery's notes, Dr Reed. She can't go to Ward Six until—'

'Yes, I'm quite aware of that. Bring them in here.'

She followed him into the now vacant room, and tried to ignore the rapid thudding of her heart as he casually pushed the door closed behind them. He took the file from her, and their fingers accidentally touched. A thrill ran through Pippa, and she was annoyed with herself. She had no right to feel like this—and he had no right to cause these feelings. Neither of them was free.

She stood motionless a few feet away as he wrote quickly with a fine-nibbed gold pen. He closed the file and stood up.

'I hope I haven't kept you from your coffee,' he said, smiling, and handed her the notes. She was struggling to retain her composure, but he was so close—she could smell his aftershave, it wasn't like Neil's, no, he wasn't like Neil at all . . .

'You won't drop it, will you?' he teased. She

38

flushed angrily. Couldn't he ever forget? 'You'll be pleased to know,' he went on, 'my toes were quite undamaged after their accident. Alas, my jacket had to go to the cleaners.'

Pippa knew she should just turn and go, and ignore his mocking remarks, but those deep blue eyes seemed to have paralysed her limbs, and she couldn't move. She could hardly breathe as she gazed up at him.

'My God, your eyes really are green!' he murmured, and rested his hands on her shoulders. His touch sent a bolt of fire through her. Her knees went weak. If only he were Neil. Neil! Heathrow. Suddenly the spell was broken.

'Is that the time? I must dash. I shan't get any coffee if I don't hurry, and I have to ring Heathrow—' She turned to go but his hands still held her.

'Heathrow? Didn't he turn up, then?'

'He? How did you know I was meeting a— he?' He was right again, of course. Infuriating!

'Wasn't it?' The corners of his mouth twitched.

'If you really want to know, although I don't know why I should tell you, I went to meet my fiancé from South America, he's coming on leave for three weeks, but there was an earthquake . . .' She waited for the inevitable sarcastic remark but it didn't come.

'Your fiancé?' His hands fell from her

shoulders.

'He's a paediatrician. We're getting married next year.'

For a moment Julian Reed stared at her. Then he strode over to the door and pulled it open, turning to say curtly, 'A doctor should know better than to fall in love with a redhead!'

He turned on his heel and went briskly along to the labour-rooms. Pippa stood in the doorway, the file against her chest, tears smarting behind her eyelids. She could still feel the pressure of his hands.

That was the second time he'd referred to her hair. All right, so he had a thing about redheads. It wasn't her fault. It didn't matter, either. Neil liked the colour of her hair, and it was Neil she was marrying, not this arrogant senior registar!

CHAPTER THREE

'I feel awful about this,' said Pippa to Lucy. They had met at lunch, and Pippa had given her the news that the Santiago flight had been delayed and was now expected at six o'clock, not five. They had gone up to their flat together, since Pippa wasn't on duty again until five, and Lucy had the rest of the day off.

Pippa felt inclined to throw off her shoes

and relax on her bed with some music and a book, but Lucy seemed keen to do some shopping, and Pippa felt it might be a good idea to join her. They needed some basic foodstuffs; coffee, cereals, bread—and, of course, milk. To her surprise, Lucy seemed reluctant.

'I had thought of shopping in London,' she said, unwilling to meet Pippa's gaze. 'I haven't been to London for ages. I could see my— friends, and it would be quite easy to meet Neil at Heathrow.'

She seemed embarrassed, and turned away to search through a kitchen drawer.

'I'm sorry, I didn't realise you'd planned on seeing your friends,' said Pippa. 'I shouldn't have landed you with meeting Neil. I feel awful about it.'

'Don't be silly. I offered. Remember?'

So she had. Now Pippa remembered. She brightened up. 'I wonder—' It was obvious to Pippa that Lucy wouldn't be able to bring back a load of groceries, but they had to be fetched. 'Could you give me a lift into the town? Those car parks are always full when I get there, and I'm not keen on the multi-storeys. I can always get the bus back.'

'Sure. Any particular place?' She seemed quite cheerful now, and her eyes sparkled.

The sun was shining, and after Lucy had dropped Pippa off at the shopping centre, or as near as possible, she sped off to London.

Pippa wondered briefly if she was still seeing the man who had so upset her—but, of course, she had no proof he had ever existed. Just her romantic imagination at work.

Basingstoke's shopping centre being an excellent one, Pippa didn't realise how the afternoon was flying past, and it wasn't until she was loaded up with two bags of groceries that she caught sight of a clock. Four-fifteen! And it was quite a walk to the bus station. To make things worse, as she hurried down the steps to the New Market Square, it began to rain, big splashy spots that presaged a heavy shower. She reached the bus station just as her bus accelerated away. A woman in a blue jacket smiled ruefully at her.

'You just missed it,' she stated unnecessarily.

'So did you.' Pippa felt cross and sounded it.

'Oh, no. I was just seeing someone off. You in a hurry?'

'Well, yes, sort of. I have to be back at work for five o'clock.'

The woman looked smug. 'Oh, dear. The next one doesn't come until quarter to. Do you have far to go?'

'Kingslake Maternity.' The woman looked interested. Oh, dear, thought Pippa, here it comes, a long saga of her births and complications . . .

'You a nurse?' It was going to be inevitable, whether she denied it or not.

42

'I'm training to be a midwife.' She was not really interested in the woman. She was wondering whether she could get a taxi, and, more important, whether she could afford one. Yet it wasn't really very far, only a couple of miles . . .

'My sister had her last baby in Kingslake,' the woman was saying. 'A little boy. She called him Damian. I told her, that was the name of the child in that horror film, you know, about the devil's child, *Omen* or something, did you see it? Mind you, he's a lovely child, bright red hair, bit like yours, all curly—'

'Is there a taxi rank near here?'

'Eh? A taxi? Oh, yes, just past the Market Square, by the cinema. You know it? As I was saying, she insisted on—'

'Sorry, I'd love to listen, but I must dash.' Pippa hurried away, leaving the woman with words still on her lips. The rain was now coming down quite heavily, and she hadn't a scarf or an umbrella, and she could imagine Sister Brayford's face if she went on duty with wet hair. But luck was with her, a black taxi was waiting. As she ran towards it, encumbered by her carrier bags, an elderly man hurried across to it, opened the door and climbed in.

Damn! Pippa could have cried as she watched it speed away towards the wet streets. There wasn't another in sight. Desperately, she pushed wet tendrils of hair off her face, looking up and down. She should have stayed in. They could have borrowed some milk. Her watch showed four-thirty. A cream-coloured car suddenly appeared from nowhere, and slowed down a few yards away. She couldn't see a 'FOR HIRE' sign, but it had to be a taxi, because other traffic didn't normally come along here. It would be more expensive than the usual sort, but what the hell? She had to get to work.

She grabbed the door as it stopped, and almost hurled herself on to the front seat. 'Kingslake Maternity Hospital, please, and I'm in a dreadful hurry.' Settling herself in the seat, she barely noticed the expensive soft grey upholstery, and the water dripping from her plastic carrier bags. She dumped the bags on the floor and fastened her seatbelt. The car increased its pace.

'Who'd have thought it would turn out so wet?' she remarked, shaking her red curls. The driver didn't speak. She noticed what nice hands he had, lean and tanned with long fingers, and she was surprised. She glanced out at the weather. The rain was not letting up. She began to realise how lucky she'd been to get this taxi. She hoped she had enough money to pay for it! Anxiously, she groped through her purse and counted what she had left after shopping. Three pounds. Would it be enough? The bus would only have been about fifty pence. It was her own fault. She shouldn't have stopped for tea and scones.

'Lucky you came by,' she said chattily, and glanced at the driver's face. All the blood in her body seemed to drain away. Except for that which flooded her face.

'Certainly was.' And for a brief moment his deep blue eyes rested on her agonised expression. His mouth twitched as she struggled to regain her composure.

'Please don't think I—I mean, I didn't know it was you—I thought you were a taxi, and I was getting desperate, I'm on duty at five—'

'You don't have to apologise,' he said easily, and his voice sent little thrills down her spine. She was acutely aware of the puddles of rainwater around her bags of shopping. She grabbed them in dismay and put them on her knees where they immediately soaked through her jeans.

'It's all right to say that, but you don't know what a mess I've made on your carpet, and my clothes have probably soaked the seat, too—'

'They'll dry. So you may as well put those bags on the floor again.' He expertly manoeuvred the Rover around a corner and a parked lorry, his lean surgeon's hands moving easily on wheel and gear lever. Pippa watched them, remembering the way they had saved a premature baby that morning. Firm, strong hands, but soft and gentle, too. They had held her shoulders, their fingers had touched . . .

She felt a flush creep up her cheeks. He

didn't seem to have noticed. She played with her bag to distract her thoughts. Julian Reed was silent.

'I hope I'm not taking you out of your way,' she said in a small voice.

'My way is your way, Nurse Garland.' He'd remembered her name!

'You're going to the hospital?'

'I work there.' He gave a crooked smile. 'Actually, I had just dropped off a couple of friends at the cinema when I saw you looking all woebegone. I'd just been to see that Stella and Amy are settled in all right. Amy gets fractious after long journeys.'

'It must be difficult, bringing up a handicapped child,' said Pippa, sympathetically. His knuckles tightened on the wheel.

'Yes. You're damned right it is. Particularly when it need not have happened.'

Pippa couldn't find the right words that wouldn't make it worse, so she said nothing.

'I thought you were going to Heathrow,' he said, his voice light. Of course, he wasn't really interested, he just needed to change the subject.

'Oh, no, the flight isn't expected until six.' He glanced at her.

'Aren't you on duty at five?'

'My friend will meet him for me. She's a staff midwife on Six.'

'Six? The pretty blonde one?' Why did she feel a surge of jealousy that he should

46

remember Lucy, too?

'That's right. Nurse Waters. How is Mrs Emery?'

'Rather too early to tell, but I don't think her kidneys have been damaged. I'm quite optimistic. She could have died, and so could the baby. But neither of them is out of the wood yet.'

The car slowed down as it reached the hospital car park. Pippa found to her surprise she didn't want it to stop. She wanted the drive to go on for ever, just the two of them . . . She gave herself a mental shake. She could not allow herself to feel like this. The car stopped. It was twenty minutes to five.

'I'm very grateful to you, Dr Reed,' Pippa began, her hand on the door-handle.

'The name's Julian.' As if she didn't know!

'I'd never have got back in time if you hadn't come along.' She grabbed the handles of her shopping bags.

'The pleasure was mine.' His voice and smile sent a shiver through her. He leaned towards her, and for a brief, heart-stopping moment she thought he was going to kiss her. But he was just reaching into the glove compartment for a bunch of keys. Blushing, Pippa clambered from the car, her knees suddenly weak, and hurried to the entrance. Her hair was still wet, and damp red tendrils clung to her cheeks.

It was only when she'd got back to her flat

and was donning a fresh white dress, that she realised she hadn't thought about this evening and Neil at all.

*   *   *

The woman on the bed cradled her new-born daughter, her eyes and cheeks glowing with happiness. All memory of the past hours of pain and discomfort was pushed into her subconscious.

'She's beautiful, Mrs Walker,' said Pippa, as she wrote the details of the birth on the notes.

'I very nearly didn't have her,' said the woman. 'I almost lost her at three months. And after four boys it would have been a disaster. I don't think I could have—'

'It's all over now, and you've got her, and she's just perfect. Now, I'll put her in the crib, and you and your husband can have a nice cup of tea.'

'Is he all right?' asked Mary Walker. 'I mean, I felt quite embarrassed, him nearly passing out like that.'

'Don't you worry, it often happens,' Pippa reassured her, placing the tiny, red-faced baby in the perspex crib. 'We all know men are the weaker sex, don't we? Even if we don't let on to them that we know.'

Mary Walker grinned, but her smile quickly disappeared as the door behind Pippa opened, and someone entered.

48

'Is that a fact?' came a deep velvet voice. Pippa, without turning, blushed to the roots of her hair. She mumbled something.

'And all these years I thought it was a secret,' said Julian Reed, peeping at the baby in the crib. Pippa and Mary grinned at each other. Pippa's pulse was racing. Even Mary could hardly take her eyes off him.

'I have found a member of the weaker sex sitting outside, looking a bit green,' said Julian. 'Does he belong to you, young lady?' He addressed Mary, who, at forty-one, was flattered to be called 'young lady'. She looked coyly at him.

'It was a bit too much for him,' she admitted. 'Poor Bill. He's never seen a baby born, and he missed this one. And it's going to be the last, I can tell you!'

'I'll send him in now then,' said the registrar. 'I see it's a girl, by the pink bracelet. And a redhead, by the looks of things.'

He gave Pippa's curls a brief tug, which made her heart lurch, and went out.

'He likes you,' said Mary. 'I'd hang on to him if I were you, he's nice. Those blue eyes—'

'He's married,' said Pippa, closing the file.

'Are you sure? He doesn't look married,' said Mary. 'And you like him too, don't you?'

Pippa was saved from answering by the entrance of Bill, looking sheepish, followed by Rosemary Parrish, one of the night staff.

'It's gone eight o'clock, Pippa,' she said,

coming across and looking at the notes.

Eight o'clock! The evening had been so busy Pippa hadn't had a chance to think about Lucy meeting Neil, and cooking him the paella in the flat. She began to feel tense, almost uncomfortable, as though anticipating an unpleasant task. But that was so silly.

'I'll take over,' said Rosemary. 'You look tired.'

That meant she looked a mess, thought Pippa. What would Neil think? She spoke briefly to the Walkers, and went off to collect her cloak.

As she walked along the corridor to the residence, her tension increased. Butterflies danced in her stomach. Of course it was due to anticipation, she told herself. Anticipation of their meeting after six months. When two people were in love, it was natural they'd feel like this. It was because she could hardly wait to see him again.

She opened the door of the flat, and hung her cloak on the hook. She could hear voices from the kitchen, the low voice of Neil, murmurs of surprise and delight from Lucy. So she was still here.

Well, of course she was here, Pippa admonished herself. She lived here. She pushed open the door and went in. They hadn't heard her enter. They sat at the kitchen table, heads together, bent over something in Neil's hand.

50

'Hi, there.' They jumped apart. Neil pushed something into his pocket. Lucy scrambled to her feet. 'Hi, Pippa. Are you early?'

'I don't think so.'

Behind the gold-rimmed spectacles, Neil's grey eyes crinkled, and a broad smile transformed his round face. The deep dimple showed in his cheek. Pippa felt a surge of affection for him. He got up, came towards her.

'I've got some letters to finish,' said Lucy, and hurried down to her room. They heard her door close. Neil took Pippa in his arms, and she waited for the earth to move. Where was the rapid thudding of her heart, the thrills up her spine when he touched her? It did happen, she'd felt it before.

'I've missed you, Pippa.' She could hear his heartbeat, too, strong and slow. She felt safe, wanted, needed. He bent his head, and his lips found hers. At first the pressure was soft, tender, then it became more demanding, more urgent. She tried her hardest to respond— What was the matter with her? She had felt the thrills, the weakness, the trembling . . .

But not with Neil.

Her mother's voice sounded in her head. Handsome is as handsome does. You can't build your life on physical attraction. There's no such thing as love at first sight. That's lust. And it doesn't last. Stick with Neil. You can trust him. You'll be safe with him. Secure.

51

Safe. Secure. It meant a lot to her mother. She was usually right. She'd been right about that fellow from the path lab. What was his name? Oh, yes, Rod. And she'd fancied she was in love with him. Love at first sight. Infatuation. Like Julian Reed.

Now her heart did begin to beat faster. Neil's arms held her tightly. She could hardly breathe. She struggled free.

'You're crushing my ribs!' she laughed.

'It's because I love you so much.'

She ran her fingers through his floppy yellow hair. He was so nice. He loved her. She mustn't forget that. She couldn't hurt him, he was too kind to hurt.

She made coffee, and they drank it in the small sitting-room. Neil told her all about Chile, and Valparaiso, the constant earthquakes.

'Hundreds every day,' he said, quite calmly, enjoying her amazement. 'Occasionally there are larger ones, around six on the Richter Scale. They can cause damage. Like the one a couple of days ago. But one gets used to them. They call them "temblors". If you can't get outside you hide under a strong table.' He laughed, and put an arm around her shoulder. Pippa tensed.

'What are you planning to do while you're home?' she asked lightly.

'Take you out. Picnics. Talk. We have a lot to talk about, Pippa.'

'Do you want more coffee?'

'No. I've got something for you.' He looked at her. 'You still wear the ring?' Pippa fingered the silver chain around her neck.

'Yes, you know I do. But it's too small for my finger. Your grandmother didn't do manual nursing work!'

'I'll get it enlarged for you. I'd like you to wear it when you're off duty. Will you?'

She knew what he meant. 'And the parents?'

'I've told my parents. Will you tell your mother? Shall we both tell her?'

Pippa took a deep breath. Her heart was thudding, for a different reason. 'Of course I will.'

He kissed her gently. 'This is for you.' He held out a small green box.

The door opened and Lucy looked in. 'Anyone want anything? I'm just going to post some letters.' They smiled refusals, and the front door closed behind her.

Pippa opened the little box. Inside lay a brooch, quite the most enchanting thing she had ever seen. On a bright copper leaf sat a tiny frog in some vivid blue stone, not sapphire.

'The leaf is Chilean copper,' Neil explained. 'The frog is Chilean lapis lazuli.'

She was lifting out the brooch as he spoke, and at the words 'lapis lazuli' she had a vision of deep blue eyes. Her hand jerked and the pin scratched her deeply. Within seconds blood had welled up.

'What have you done?' He grabbed her hand. She dabbed at the scratch with a tissue.

'It's nothing. I just caught it on the pin. I'll get a plaster.'

'Let me.'

'It's all right. I know where they are.' Rummaging through the bathroom cabinet, she inwardly cursed Julian Reed. Even from a distance he was bothering her. Now look what he had made her do! There were no small plasters. The scratch was a deep one, and wouldn't stop bleeding. If Lucy were here, she'd have some plasters. Surely she wouldn't mind if she took one? Pippa knew where they were kept, in a shoe box in a cupboard. She could be ages coming back from the postbox. No, she wouldn't mind, they often went into each other's rooms. She pushed open the door and went in.

The room was untidy, it always was. Organised in her working life, Lucy was the opposite in private. Pippa opened the cupboard and a glove fell out. She lifted out the shoe box. It was full of oddments, old letters, hair rollers, reels of thread, scissors. She found the plasters and stuck one over the scratch. Putting the box back, she noticed the corner of a letter, with a strange yet familiar stamp on it. Chile. One of her letters? What was Lucy doing with one of her letters from Neil? She pulled it out. It was from Neil. His name, in small neat handwriting, was on the back. Valparaiso, Chile. She turned it over, puzzled. Why should Lucy—? But it wasn't one of her own letters. The name and address was quite plain.

Miss Lucy Waters, Pippa read. Flat Seven, Staff Residence, Kingslake Maternity Hospital. It was postmarked several weeks ago.

CHAPTER FOUR

Pippa closed the door behind Neil, and he left to go across to the doctors' residence, where he was staying with a friend, a medical colleague. It was too late for him to go all the way home to Romsey, where his parents lived; he didn't like disturbing them. He would go there the next day and take his luggage.

Pippa realised how much she must mean to him, if he could put off going home until he'd seen her. She had met his parents, and had seen what a dominant personality his mother, Isobel, had. For some reason she had seemed to like Pippa, and that in turn seemed to influence Neil. He'd never mentioned any other serious girlfriends to Pippa. Perhaps he'd never had any. Casual friendships she knew about, mostly nurses he had met in the course of his work. He'd taken Lucy out a few times.

Lucy had gone to bed, and, as Pippa passed her closed door, she thought again of the letter from Neil. Why should he write to Lucy? But Pippa couldn't mention it to either of them. She would have to wait until she was told. If she ever was. There had to be a logical explanation. Lucy must have written to him first. She knew his address in Chile.

Pippa recalled the brief look of panic in Lucy's eyes when she'd told her she'd taken a sticking plaster for her finger.

'I hope you don't mind, Lucy, but I knew you wouldn't want to come back and find me lying on the floor, bleeding to death.'

Lucy had laughed, but the laugh hadn't reached her eyes. 'Of course I don't mind,' she'd said quickly.

'I'll stock up the cabinet next time I go shopping,' said Pippa. 'Plasters aren't things one puts on the grocery list, are they?'

She lay in bed in the darkness, trying to sleep. But there were so many questions. About Neil, about Lucy, about herself. About Julian Reed with the kissable mouth, the deep blue eyes—those lapis lazuli eyes—a frog brooch—lapis lazuli . . . She fell asleep.

Next day she had a straight shift but Lucy had a day off, so Pippa didn't disturb her when she got ready for duty. In Sister's office, Annette Foster was dabbing perfume behind her ears, and she started when Pippa came into the room.

'You're early,' she said accusingly.

'Am I? A couple of minutes.' She sat down, and was soon joined by the rest of the morning shift.

Pippa was given two routine patients, a marked contrast to yesterday morning when she had been put in charge of Diane Emery. She wondered briefly how she was, and if the baby was still surviving. She could ask someone, Julian Reed perhaps. Her cheeks grew warm at the thought.

She went into the first of her patients, a mother of two. Sheila Treadgold. Sheila was puffing away quite happily, humming a tune, as she'd been taught, determined not to have any pain-killing drugs. All Pippa had to do was record her blood-pressure, time her contractions, and listen to the foetal heart. She'd be quite a while yet. The last examination had revealed her to be still at an early stage.

She went into Gail Carey, a newly married girl of twenty, who had already been in labour for fifteen hours. Oh well, she'll be delivering soon, no doubt, thought Pippa.

Gail looked pale and tired. 'Oh, someone else,' she said wearily. 'I'm getting tired of all the new faces. Like a circus. Who are you?'

'I'm the midwife who is going to look after you until you have your baby. It's the shift changeover, you see.'

'P. Garland,' said Gail, reading her name

badge. 'What's the P for?'

'Philippa, but I'm called Pippa. And I don't expect you'll get to know me very well. This baby must be nearly ready to make his entrance.'

'They said that last night when I came in, but he doesn't seem too keen. Can't blame him really. They say birth is very traumatic for a baby. If he is a he. Could be a she, I suppose.'

She licked her lips, and Pippa passed her a glass of water. The girl's mouth seemed dry, and, after her brief examination, Pippa realised this baby had still a long way to go before he reached the correct anterior position for delivery. And after fifteen hours Gail was already very distressed. Pippa put on a cheerful smile.

'The baby seems to be taking his time. How are you coping?'

'I'm tired. I didn't think it would take so long. My friend was only eight hours. Mind you, she had a forceps delivery. Would that help me? Is the baby stuck, or something?'

'He's not stuck,' said Pippa. 'But he's got to turn round yet. About the forceps, well, that depends on how quickly he turns. You've got a long way to go.'

'Can I have some more pethidine, then? I've had two, I think. I didn't fancy an epidural. I'm a coward.'

Her dark hair clung damply to her neck.

Pippa listened to the baby's heart, which was a little rapid. Yet everything else seemed normal. Pippa read the notes thoroughly. She didn't want to miss anything important. Gail was two weeks premature, and labour had started with rupture of the membranes. This happened because the head was high. It was on the cards that it would be a long labour. Could Gail take it? And supposing the baby became distressed?

As an afterthought, she glanced at the bottom bed sheet before she left. An ominous greenish stain had appeared. She went out to find Sister. Annette Foster was nowhere to be found, but Sister Brayford was in her office, the door half open. She was talking to someone. She noticed Pippa as she hesitated in the doorway.

'Come in, Nurse Garland. Is something wrong?'

Pippa went into the room, and the person behind the door became visible. Blushing, and trying to stop it, Pippa told her about Gail.

'Early foetal distress, you think? I'd better come and check.'

'Not surprised,' said Julian Reed, and looked straight at Pippa. Her heart, already beating fast, threatened to run away with her.

'Occipito-posteriors are always a problem,' said Sister.

'Unless they deliver as posteriors,' said Julian. 'If we don't do something with this one we'll have another Mrs Linney.'

Pippa recalled the deep transverse arrest of yesterday. Fortunately, it had turned out well, after a difficult forceps delivery. But this baby was distressed—was there time? Julian Reed seemed to read her thoughts.

'You're right,' he said, as if she'd spoken aloud. 'We may have to move quickly.'

'It's not as urgent as all that, surely?' protested Sister. 'If we can wait until the head has rotated—'

'I don't like waiting, while a baby is suffering,' said Julian curtly. 'I'll just check Mrs Lewis, so let me know about Mrs Carey straight away.'

He left the room, and Sister glanced at Pippa's pink cheeks.

'Warm, Nurse Garland? You haven't got a temperature? There's a lot of summer flu around.'

'Oh, no, Sister. I'm fine.' She followed her back to Gail who was lying with her eyes closed.

'I think I need another injection, Sister,' she said wearily. 'The contractions are really strong, all in my back as well.'

'We'll see,' said Sister, listening to the baby's heartbeat. 'Has your husband been to see you?'

'He's been here all night. He's gone to get something to eat.'

Sister nodded to Pippa. 'It is raised. So is

her pulse. I'd better check the stage of dilation, although I doubt she's anywhere near ready.' She spoke quietly, but Gail heard her and groaned.

'How much longer, Sister? I feel exhausted.'

'Don't worry,' said Sister, pulling on sterile gloves. After a deft examination she straightened up. 'Six centimetres. She's got four to go. Go and tell Dr Reed, will you, Nurse Garland?'

'Yes, Sister.'

'Tell him, definitely fresh meconium, foetal heart raised.'

'Yes, Sister.'

Breathing quickly, Pippa went around the rooms, until she found the room where Mrs Lewis was being prepared for induction. Annette Foster frowned when Pippa entered, but Julian turned to her with a smile. He has lovely teeth, she thought inconsequentially.

'Excuse me, Dr Reed—' One eyebrow lifted slightly.

'Mrs Carey?'

'She's six centimetres dilated, and there's fresh meconium. Foetal heart is a hundred and sixty.'

'I'll come right away.'

'What about the induction, Dr Reed?' asked Sister Foster.

'Get Dr Wilson,' said Julian, crossing to the door. 'He's extremely competent. And he's around somewhere. Checking the twins lady.'

'I see. Very well.'

Pippa could hardly keep up with his long stride. They went into Gail's room, and Pippa couldn't help but admire the way he reassured the frightened girl, and the way his hands carefully checked the position of the baby. He sat on the edge of the bed, and laid a hand on Gail's.

'Your baby is making rather heavy weather of this situation,' he said softly. Pippa almost wished she were Gail. 'I don't think we can leave it any longer.'

'That's a load off my mind,' said Gail. 'Can you do something?'

'Well, if you were a little further on we could do a vacuum extraction. Have you heard of that?'

'Sounds like a Hoover.' She giggled weakly. Julian grinned.

'And if you were further on than that we could do a forceps delivery.'

'My friend had one of those,' said Gail.

'But, in your case,' he went on, 'it's too early for either of those. The cervix just isn't dilated enough. So I'm afraid the only thing we can do is a Caesarean section.'

Gail's eyes were dark as she sank back against the pillows.

'It's the only thing, Gail. The only way to save your baby.'

Pippa liked the way he used her first name. She liked the way he treated her as an intelligent human being. She liked the way he worked. She liked—oh, everything about him—his eyes, his mouth, his voice. His voice made her melt inside.

'Well, Gail?'

Pippa wondered if the girl felt all weak inside, as she did. No, she seemed too tired to care. She just wanted it to be over.

'I'll do whatever you advise, Doctor,' said Gail. 'I can't carry on like this much longer—oh—here's another one—' She closed her eyes and her jaw tensed. Julian patted her hand and stood up.

'Of course you can't.' He turned to Sister Brayford. 'I'll get it organised straight away. Is the theatre free?'

'Yes, they've finished Mrs Burton. She's in recovery.'

'Shall we say twenty minutes?'

'I should think that could be done.'

He gave Pippa a long look and turned to go. Gail opened her eyes.

'Are you going to do it, Doctor?' she asked.

'Naturally. I wouldn't let anyone else do it.' He spoke seriously, and for a moment Pippa wondered why he wanted it done so quickly. Most doctors had a policy of 'wait and see'. Yet Julian hadn't even hesitated. And he was doing it himself, not delegating it to a junior registrar.

Gail sighed. 'I shall be glad when it's over,' she said. 'If my husband comes back in time, may he come and—?'

'See the birth?' said Julian. 'I'm sorry. Not for a Caesarean.'

'But I must have someone there with me! Someone I trust.'

'Then why not our redheaded Nurse Garland here?' suggested Julian, ruffling Pippa's hair. Pippa went pink, and tried to ignore the thudding of her heart.

'There will be nurses there with you,' she said awkwardly. 'And you don't really know me—Æ

'I like you,' said Gail simply. 'Please—will you stay with me?'

'I think we can manage that,' said Sister Brayford. She turned to Pippa. 'Mrs Treadgold will be some time yet. I'll keep an eye on her while you're away.'

'Thank you, Sister. It's a long time since I saw my first Caesarean.'

'Well—I didn't mean for you to stay to the end . . .' She glanced at Gail. 'Oh, very well, since your other patient is only at the beginning. But don't take advantage of it. When it's over, straight down to coffee, and back.'

'Yes, Sister.'

'I'll get you a consent form to sign, Mrs Carey. I'll be right back.'

Pippa was churning inside. She was going to watch Julian Reed operate, she was going to watch those long gentle fingers at work again.

64

She found herself staring at his hands as he opened the door, and turned away guiltily. She had been imagining those same hands touching her. And her cheeks flamed.

Soon Gail was nicely sedated, and waiting in the ante-room before the operation. Meanwhile, Pippa got gowned up in the nurses' changing room. Staff Midwife Charles was to be the 'runner', and she was putting on her greens at the same time. As Pippa slipped out of her white dress, Nurse Charles turned as she reached the door to theatre. She opened it, and said in a clear voice, 'Jewellery, Nurse Garland?'

Pippa's hand went to the silver chain and ring around her neck.

'No—it isn't jewellery—not really—'

Leaving the door half open, Nurse Charles came across and looked at it. 'It's a ring. An engagement ring, isn't it? So you're engaged at last. When's the happy day?'

Through the crack of the door, Pippa could see Julian Reed scrubbing up at the sink. Covered with confusion, she mumbled something about not deciding yet.

'It's Neil Chappell, isn't it? The paediatric bod. Mother's boy. Well, well, fancy you hooking him. I'd heard something about it. Thought it couldn't be true. Isn't he in South Africa or somewhere?'

Her voice was clear, and it carried. Julian hadn't paused in his ablutions. Pippa watched the crack of the door anxiously.

'He's in Chile. South America,' she said, wishing this conversation were going on anywhere but here. 'Actually, he's home on leave at the moment.'

'Well, well, lucky you! Hope his mother likes you. She didn't like any of the others.'

Fastening her mask over her ears, she went out of the room. Miserably, Pippa put on her own and followed her.

The operation began. Gail was given oxygen, then a light anaesthetic—not too light or she could wake during the procedure, but not enough to depress the baby's breathing.

Pippa watched Julian's hands as he made the first incision across the taut skin of the abdomen. They moved surely and confidently, with no hesitation. She knew she'd feel quite safe if he had to perform the same operation on herself. She would happily put her own and her baby's life in his hands. Then she flushed as she realised what she was thinking. A Caesarean meant a baby. Whose baby? Neil's? Well, naturally. He'd want children. He was a children's doctor. And she'd be quite happy having children. Her mother would be delighted. And Neil's parents were quite elderly; they could probably hardly wait to become grandparents.

With a start, Pippa suddenly realised how the operation was progressing. The uterus had been opened, and inside the amniotic sac the

66

baby could just be seen. As the sac was punctured the water gushed out. Very carefully, Julian's gloved hands slowly withdrew the head of the baby, and then its body.

'Time nine twenty-five,' said Theatre Sister in a clear voice, and it was noted on the chart. The baby wriggled, opened its mouth, and Nurse Charles sucked out any mucus. It screwed up its face and a cry filled the room. The cord was cut, and Pippa noticed it was a girl.

The baby was wrapped in a cellular blanket and passed to the waiting paediatrician. All that remained to be done was the removal of the afterbirth and the suturing.

'I am about to close the uterus,' Julian said, glancing up. 'Please check the swabs.'

Sister counted, Nurse Charles counted, and Pippa realised they were waiting for her to count them, too. Julian was frowning, his hand with forceps and needle poised over the open incision. She counted quickly, and must have said the correct number because Julian nodded and began to sew. It was all over now. The baby would go up to the ward with Gail, providing all was well. She would be kept quiet for twenty-four hours, before being handled and bathed. Gail was soon in the recovery room, and starting to wake. She looked up at Pippa, grimaced and tried to smile.

'Over?' she croaked, her throat dry from the

tube.

'All over,' said Pippa. 'You've got a little girl.'

Gail sighed, gave a contented smile, and her eyes closed.

'She'll stay here for a little while,' said Theatre Sister. 'You'd better go back to Delivery Suite now.'

'Yes. Thank you.' She glanced at Gail, but the girl was deeply asleep. She hurried away. Halfway to Delivery Suite she remembered Sister's instructions to go to coffee. She turned on her heel, and collided with a white coat. The hands which grasped her shoulders were strong.

'You do make a habit of it, don't you?' Julian teased, and colour flooded her cheeks. She wished she could stop this adolescent blushing every time he spoke to her.

'I just remembered,' she said, unable to find a caustic reply. 'I'm supposed to be going to coffee.'

'So you are. I wish I could join you, but I just don't have time, and anyway, you also have a habit of throwing hot coffee around, don't you?'

'That's a bit unfair!' she protested. 'It only happened once, and that was your fault!'

'Mine?'

His hands still held her shoulders, and she couldn't help but look into those deep blue eyes. She was remembering her conversation

68

with Nurse Charles. He must have overheard it. What was he thinking?

'You just did it again—came up behind me so quietly,' she said, aware of the rapid thudding of her heart. Surely he could hear it!

'If I remember correctly, you were just standing there with a vague smile on your face. Daydreaming, no doubt. You'll have to watch that.'

'I don't daydream—' she burst out, remembering she'd been doing just that during the operation. 'I don't daydream—ever!' she repeated vehemently, and stepped back so he had to drop his hands.

'You never daydream?' he said softly, so she could hardly hear. 'Don't you ever dream of your fiancé? Didn't you ever dream of the day he'd be home from Chile? Of wearing his ring on your finger, not round your neck?'

'How dare you?' Her cheeks were flaming now, not from embarrassment but from anger. Not only had he heard the conversation in theatre, he had seen her.

'Perhaps you don't daydream about him. Perhaps you're not really in love with him at all.'

'That's nothing to do with you!'

He moved closer, and for a moment she was transfixed by the expression in his eyes. Then she recalled what he'd said. Angrily, she turned and stalked away down the corridor, breathing hard. Her pulse was racing, and she could still feel the pressure of his hands on her arms, still see the teasing twinkle in his blue eyes. This time he had really overstepped the mark. Of course she was in love with Neil.

Why had Julian Reed come to this hospital, upsetting everything? She'd been happy with Neil, looking forward to a calm, ordered existence in the future. She didn't need any blue-eyed married man to come along and spoil things.

She hurried along to the reception area and the lifts. A few people were seated at the little white tables, talking. One woman sat alone, looking around her expectantly. Waiting for someone. When she caught Pippa's eye she got up quickly. With a start, Pippa recognised Stella, Julian's wife.

'Hello.' Stella crossed the floor towards her, and Pippa felt it would be rude to ignore her. She didn't know her, she was reluctant to talk to her, but the woman had taken her part in the argument at the airport. So she smiled.

'Hello. It's Stella, isn't it?'

'Fancy you remembering my name! I'm afraid I don't know yours.' Her eyes alighted on the name badge on Pippa's dress.

'Pippa Garland.'

'You work here then?'

'I'm a pupil midwife.'

'It must have been a shock to find Julian working here, too,' said Stella. 'After that fuss he made at Heathrow. I take it you have met him here?'

'Oh, yes,' said Pippa grimly. 'I've met him all right.'

'Oh, dear, as bad as that, is it? He can be rather critical, I'm afraid.'

'Look, I can't really stop to talk . . .' Besides, she didn't want to talk about Julian Reed. Not to Stella, anyway. Why, she didn't know.

'No, you must be busy,' said Stella. 'I was hoping to catch Julian for a moment, but I suppose he's busy, too.'

'He's just done a Caesarean,' said Pippa. 'I'm not sure whether he'll have time to go down for coffee.' Stella looked puzzled. 'Look,' said Pippa impulsively. 'I'm going down now, why don't you come with me? If he should turn up—if not, I'll give him a message.'

'That's kind of you.'

They started down the stairs, the lift being in use. Stella glanced at Pippa.

'You don't sound like Olivia, you know. But you really look like her. You're her spitting image. He must have told you.'

'We haven't had that sort of conversation,' said Pippa stiffly.

'No, of course not. Purely professional, I expect.'

'Sort of.'

'He's got this thing about redheads, you see,' said Stella, quite chattily, as they walked along to the dining-room. She was wearing a

71

pretty blue jogging suit, and her dark hair framed her attractive face. She had lovely deep blue eyes too, Pippa noticed with a shock.

'Doesn't it bother you, all this Olivia stuff?' asked Pippa. 'I mean, if she was his girlfriend—'

'Fiancée,' Stella corrected her. 'Is this the place?'

'How can you talk about her so easily?' said Pippa. 'I mean, he must be over redheads by now, since he married you, and now you've got Amy—'

Stella stopped in her tracks and looked at Pippa. Her eyes widened. 'So that was what you meant at the airport!' she exclaimed. 'You thought I was married to Julian! Pippa, hasn't he told you? He's not my husband—he's my brother!'

CHAPTER FIVE

For a moment Pippa felt stunned. She stared at Stella, recognising the deep blue eyes and dark wavy hair. She should have seen the similarity before. But she'd been too angry at the airport, too humiliated.

'I didn't know,' she said lamely. 'Julian never mentioned it.'

'It wouldn't occur to him,' said Stella, as they entered the large dining-room. Joining thc short queue, collecting coffee and finding space to sit, they were unable to talk until they were seated, their coffee on the table between them. They'd been lucky to get an alcove to themselves.

Pippa was feeling very strange inside, surprised and excited. She felt as though something momentous were about to happen.

'We've been very close,' Stella explained as they sipped their coffee. 'I'm older than Julian by three years, and after our mother died, when Julian was only thirteen, I sort of had to take over her duties.' She gave a little laugh. 'Not that he really needed mothering. He's always been very self-sufficient.'

'I can imagine,' said Pippa, wondering why she had butterflies in her stomach. She hadn't wanted to talk about him at first. But things were different now.

'He decided he was going to be a doctor at an early age, sure he could cure people of cancer one day. Our mother died of cancer. She was only forty-three. Well, of course, he soon began to realise it wouldn't be as easy as that. And by then I was married to Drew.'

She paused, looked at her hands, swirled her coffee in the cup.

'Are you divorced?' asked Pippa gently. She knew from experience that sometimes a handicapped child could cause friction between parents. Or else draw them closer.

'Goodness, no,' said Stella, her eyes bright.

'No, Drew was killed in a motorway pile-up three years ago.'

'Oh.' Pippa's immediate surge of sympathy was over-ridden by a surge of curiosity. Her pulses quickened. 'Not the one at Markfield, on the M1?' There must have been a number of motorway accidents three years ago. What had made her think it would be that one? Simply because she had good reason to remember that particular accident.

'Why—yes! Did you treat the casualties at your hospital?'

'Oh, no, nothing like that. I just—remember it.'

'Drew had gone with a colleague to a dental conference in Sheffield. They were returning home. An articulated lorry was going too fast.'

Pippa stared at her. Her eyes were dark with remembered pain.

'A dental conference?'

'At Sheffield. Is something wrong?'

'It's just that—my father was killed in that accident. And he had been to a dental conference—he was a dentist

Stella was peering at her name badge. She let out a deep breath.

'I thought your surname was just coincidence. Was Ian Garland your father?'

Pippa nodded. 'My parents were divorced.'

'Yes, of course. I knew Kay was his second wife. So you're his daughter. Fancy that. You're very much like him.'

74

'Did you know him well?' asked Pippa, trying to recover from her second shock that day.

'Very well. They were partners. Drew, Ian, and James Thorpe. Poor James. He had to struggle on alone for a while.'

They drank their coffee without speaking.

'Of course,' said Stella, changing the subject, 'it was my having Amy that changed Julian's course of career. He was going to be a cancer surgeon. But then he saw what happened to me and Amy, and he decided he was going to be an obstetrician.'

'What happened to Amy?' asked Pippa politely, almost knowing the answer as she spoke.

'Well, I'm not medically qualified, but Julian did try to explain it to me. Apparently the cord prolapsed, but the junior doctor who was in charge didn't recognise it, and it was only when there were strong signs of severe distress that he did a forceps delivery. Julian said he should have done an immediate Caesarean.'

'Ah,' said Pippa. That explained his lack of hesitation in deciding to do a Caesarean on Gail Carey. She'd thought at the time he was being rather hasty, but now she knew why. Better to be safe than sorry, must be his motto. In fact, Gail's baby had seemed to be in remark-ably good condition, despite the distress. 'Don't you feel angry?' she asked Stella.

'Angry?'

'That it could have been avoided.'

'Well, of course I was. I was furious at the time. When they told me she would always be handicapped I could have screamed. But anger wouldn't have solved anything, and now I suppose I've come to terms with it. I wouldn't be without her. And, despite what people say, Amy does get a lot of fun from life. She's a happy child.'

Pippa was beginning to admire Stella more and more. Not only did she have a helpless child to care for, but she had no husband to help her. Yet there were no sounds of discontent, no grudges harboured.

'Tell me more about Olivia,' she asked impulsively. 'Is she pretty?'

'Very pretty. Like a chocolate box. Julian absolutely adored her. They were engaged, but she married—' She stopped, and coloured guiltily. She half rose from her seat. 'Julian! I wondered if you'd make it. Pippa said you were busy.'

Julian glanced briefly at Pippa and said, 'She's quite right. I haven't really got the time. But Kit Butler said he'd seen you here so I thought I'd better come and see what you wanted.' He kissed his sister on the cheek and sat beside Pippa, whose heart unaccountably began to race. Oh, this was so stupid! Just because the man had sat by her. She moved fractionally away. It was worse now than

76

before, when she'd thought he was married. Then she'd had a good reason for trying to keep her feelings in check. Now it seemed they were out of control, but she had to resist them, for Neil's sake. She moved to go.

'Are you leaving us, Nurse Garland?'

'Julian,' Stella interrupted. 'Did you know Pippa is Ian Garland's daughter?'

'The name rang a bell.'

He turned and looked at her, and she felt herself sinking, drowning under that lapis lazuli gaze. Her heart was galloping away, and her palms were damp.

'I hadn't seen him since I was small,' said Pippa weakly.

'I didn't know he had a daughter, particularly such an attractive one,' said Julian, still watching her. 'And you know how I feel about redheads, Stella.'

Was he teasing? thought Pippa. Or warning her off?

'I have to go back on duty,' she said stiffly. 'Will you excuse me?' Julian moved his long legs to allow her to pass, but she was acutely aware of the nearness of him.

'Mrs Treadgold is still puffing and panting,' he said.

She smiled, and as she left she heard Stella say, 'I had a phone call this morning, Julian. The Foresters have invited us to a meal tomorrow evening. Can you make it?'

Pippa went slowly back to the Delivery

Suite, still wondering about Olivia. All she knew was that Julian must have loved her very deeply.

*   *   *

As the days passed, Pippa grew more determined not to let Julian Reed affect her feelings for Neil. She had little chance to see her fiancé, with her long hours of duty, except for the occasional evening out—once to the theatre in London, another time to a riverside pub.

Lucy seemed to be acting very strangely, too, and Pippa put it down to Mike Badger's leaving. Unless she, too, had fallen under Julian's spell. She had an advantage there over Pippa; she wasn't a redhead.

Pippa still hadn't got round to mentioning the letter from Neil to Lucy; in fact, she'd hardly thought about it. She couldn't ask Lucy. Could she ask Neil? In fact, ought she to ask him? There shouldn't be any secrets between them, not if they were planning to get married.

Neil had told quite a few people of their engagement. Pippa knew this without being told, as word had soon spread around, and everyone kept asking her if they were holding a party. With Neil having less than three weeks' leave, Pippa felt there wasn't time for parties but was that her real reason? Neil was talking about holding one next week.

On Monday Pippa had a day off, and they had planned to visit her mother. The day dawned bright and warm, and Pippa wore a dress she knew Neil liked, a cotton one with a full skirt, with a design of sprigs of pink daisies and green leaves.

Lucy put her head round her bedroom door and said she hoped Pippa would have a good time, then hurried off to Ward Six. She hadn't dawdled, as she usually did; she had seemed extra keen to get on duty. Pippa wondered again what was wrong. Another case of unrequited love? She knew some girls were prone to this sort of thing. There had been a girl doing her general training with Pippa, named Celia, who did nothing but fall in love with married doctors or men who were oblivious to her charms, and she was constantly wailing, to anyone who'd listen, how it was real love this time, and what could she do? She had eventually eloped with one of the patients—a married man, naturally. Pippa often wondered what had happened to them.

Could Lucy be another Celia? She certainly didn't seem to be quite as irresponsible as Celia. Although, Pippa suddenly realised, she didn't know Lucy at all. Lucy never seemed to show her deeper feelings. What could she be hiding behind that normally cheerful façade?

But Pippa was determined not to let Lucy spoil her day out. She stepped into Neil's hired Volvo, and moaned again about exchanging her blue Ford Escort.

'It's not going to last much longer, Neil,' she insisted. 'It makes some awful noises.'

'I expect you've worn it out,' he said teasingly.

'Well, I've seen a smashing red Astra in the town—I wish I could get it. I suppose I could get a loan from the bank—'

'What's the point, Pippa?' He was frowning. 'You won't be here to use it. You'll be in Chile in six months' time.'

'Six months is a long time,' she said lightly, hoping she didn't sound flippant. 'Anything can happen in six months.'

Neil glanced at her, still frowning. 'What do you mean, Pippa?'

'Well—I suppose I could fail my exams. Or something,' she said lamely.

'Oh. But you won't, you know you won't. For a moment I thought you meant us.'

'Don't be silly.' She flashed him a smile which he didn't notice as he negotiated a bend.

'Your mother is the last one to tell,' Neil reminded her as they drove along.

'To tell?' said Pippa, pretending not to understand.

'About the engagement. That is why we're visiting her, isn't it?'

'I'm not sure. I do visit her because she's my mother, you know.'

Neil didn't answer, and drove carefully around a parked car. Pippa vaguely recalled the excuses she'd made to Lucy, that she didn't want anyone to know until the parents had been told. And she could easily have rung her mother, or written to her, to tell her the news. Why had she waited? It was a few days since Neil had come home. She should have told her mother. She knew she'd be overjoyed. So why had she been so reluctant?

They passed through Liss, and soon they were on the outskirts of Petersfield. Neil was chatting about Chile—how she'd love it there, the hospital was great, and so were the other members of staff. He now spoke Spanish quite well. Pippa groaned inwardly. Languages had never been her strong point. She could manage school French, and a few words of other European languages picked up on holiday, but that was all.

They started down the narrow road that led to Steep, the village where her mother lived. Pippa couldn't understand why she felt so apprehensive, even sick inside. Neil drew up outside the picturesque thatched cottage and turned off the engine.

'Well. We're here,' said Pippa brightly, getting out. She waited at the little white gate.

'I love this cottage,' said Neil. Pippa stared at him in amazement.

'This tiny cottage? But it doesn't compare with your parents' house in Romsey.'

'That's what I mean. That's too big, too impersonal. I can imagine us living in a cottage

81

like this. Two of us, then three, four, possibly more.'

'Hey, hey! Don't forget who has the babies!'

'I took it for granted you'd want children,' he said, his hand on the gate.

'I do, I do, but I don't like being taken for granted.' She caught sight of his hurt expression. 'I'm sorry, Neil. Just don't rush me.' She strode up the path between the delphiniums and hollyhocks. 'And, anyway,' she continued, 'how would we live in the country, if you're working as a consultant paediatrician?'

'I may decide to become a plain GP,' he said, but before he could enlarge on it, the front door was opened and Pippa's mother stood smiling on the doorstep.

Eleanor Garland was not a particularly attractive woman, but her large deep brown eyes and finely marked eyebrows made people look twice. Her fair hair was fading now, at forty-seven, and had lost the golden glints of her youth.

She hugged and kissed Pippa, and kissed Neil, too. Pippa immediately realised she knew why they were both there. She seemed to be full of suppressed excitement.

'Come in, come in, don't mind the mess, sit down, I'll make some tea. Or would you rather have coffee?'

They sat in the small cosy sitting-room, surrounded by pine picture frames, sprays of dried pressed flowers, and half-finished pictures. This was Eleanor's way of supplementing her income, not that she needed the money. She made dried flower pictures and bookmarks for the tourist trade. She sold them in Reading, Portsmouth, Southampton, and Winchester, and she supplied the local shops, too. Although Ian had always made sure she was well provided for, she liked to feel independent.

'Can't sit and do nothing,' she often said. 'Not in my nature.'

She brought in a tray of coffee and gipsy creams, and put it on a small table.

Although they chatted easily about Chile, and life in Steep village, and Pippa's training, underneath it Pippa felt tense and awkward. They finished the coffee, Neil had the last biscuit—Pippa had a sudden recollection of Julian refusing chocolate biscuits from Annette Foster, because he never ate between meals—and Eleanor offered more. They both refused.

'I'll wash up,' Pippa said, jumping up.

'No, it's all right—'

'Please.' She took the tray into the small kitchen, and soon had the hot water running. She supposed Neil would be telling her mother the news. But perhaps he was waiting for her to do it. As she placed the pretty china cups on the rack, a door opened and closed behind her.

'What's wrong?' asked Eleanor in a quiet voice. Pippa glanced anxiously at the door. 'It's all right, Neil's upstairs. Now, Pippa, what is it?'

'I don't know what you mean.'

'You've been on edge ever since you arrived,' said Eleanor. 'You and Neil haven't had a row, have you?'

'Goodness me, no. We never argue. Perhaps we ought to . . .'

'What does that mean?'

'I don't know. Please don't ask me.' She turned to face her mother. 'We came to give you some news, Mother.'

'You're going to Chile?'

'Eventually, I suppose,' she said slowly.

'So you're going to marry Neil. I always knew you would. I'm so happy for you, Pippa. You were made for each other.'

'Surely you don't believe in all that, Mother. You've always said—'

'I know what I've always said. And I shall say it again. Never marry for looks, and love at first sight. It doesn't exist. It's lust. And it doesn't last.'

'Mother, just because you and Dad—'

'Well, I'm not denying it's because your father and I split up. I wouldn't make such statements if I didn't know they were true. Look at me, Pippa. I'm forty-seven and I look old—yes, I do, because I was left to bring up a child on my own. I didn't have parents to help

84

me. I had to do it all alone. While he—went off with a pretty little floozie who held his instruments for him and gazed into his eyes.'

'Please, Mother, keep your voice down.'

'I'm sorry, Pippa. Neil has to know how I feel. How bitter your father made me. Just because I made the mistake of falling for a pair of blue eyes and a charming manner.'

For a brief moment Pippa saw a pair of blue eyes in her mind, and she shivered. She felt she was betraying herself.

'That wasn't the only reason you parted,' she said. 'Not just because he was good-looking.'

'If he hadn't been so handsome and charming that other little floozie wouldn't have thrown herself at him,' said Eleanor, sitting down. 'If he'd been fat or bald . . .'

Pippa gripped the tea towel in her fists. They had this conversation nearly every time she came home. She'd heard it most of her life. 'There had to be more than that,' she repeated grimly. 'Don't forget, he gave me up, too.'

'Yes, and that I could never forgive. Not once did he come back to see you.'

'It must have broken his heart,' said Pippa. 'He must have had his reasons.'

'Reasons? Oh yes, he had plenty of excuses. Felt it would cause you more harm if he kept coming and going. Some reason!'

Pippa sat down and faced her mother. She spoke softly. 'Mother—could it have been

85

because he loved me so much? Because it would have broken his heart to leave me again and again?'

Eleanor's eyes were bright. 'Are you on his side now? The father who abandoned you?'

'No, no, it's not that. I'm just trying to see both sides, that's all. There have to be two sides to an argument.'

'Well, in our divorce there was only one that I could see. He walked out on us, and left us to our fate.'

'Oh, Mother that isn't true!' Pippa protested. 'You know he always made sure we didn't go short financially. He bought you this cottage—'

'Money isn't everything,' said Eleanor shortly. She got up. 'Still, if you are so sure he was nearly perfect—'

'I didn't say that. He did let us down. I admit that. But it could have been a lot worse.'

'Could it? Well, he's dead now and we'll never know his real reasons, shall we? Now let's talk about you and Neil. When are you planning to get married?'

'I don't know. We haven't really discussed it.' She hung the tea towel on a plate rack.

'When does he have his next leave?' Eleanor removed the tea towel and hung it on a hook.

'January. For a month.'

'Well, that's ideal! Three weeks for the banns—'

'Please, Mother, don't rush me. Everyone's rushing me!'

'Well, you'll be qualified by then. Why wait? He's a nice steady young man, and he adores you. He'll go far. Why hanker after the moon?'

Pippa stared at her. 'What do you mean?'

'If you wait for someone like your father to come along and sweep you off your feet, let me tell you, it won't work. They think too much of themselves, they think they can crook their little fingers . . .'

Pippa sighed. Crook their little fingers, hold your shoulders, ruffle your hair. Was she asking for the moon? She nodded. He wouldn't want her anyway, he'd just string her along, waiting for someone who didn't have red hair like Olivia . . .

'You're probably right, Mother,' she said quietly. 'I suppose January will be as good a time as any to get married.'

CHAPTER SIX

January was six months away, but to Pippa it could have been tomorrow. It was too soon. And she felt her mother had talked her into it. Her mother was right, of course, she always was. Neil was safe and steady, and he loved her. And at least she wasn't infatuated with him. But January!

87

Neil was anxious to visit the vicar of the church in Steep, wanted to go right away to get it organised, but Pippa had persuaded him to wait a few days. He still had plenty of time left. Or was she secretly hoping there wouldn't be time, that they'd have to put it off until next summer? She was feeling so confused, she didn't know what to think.

She went on duty the next day with a feeling of dread, she didn't know why. Neil was organising a party for Friday night, and he'd asked her to invite all her colleagues and friends. Having worked at Kingslake until last Christmas, Neil already knew most of the permanent staff. Pippa's heart gave a lurch. Would he ask Julian? Had they met? Perhaps she ought to ask him. And perhaps he would make some excuse not to go. That would be easier all round. The thought of asking him both repelled and attracted her. It wouldn't come as a surprise to him. She had already told him about Neil, that day in the doctors' office. And he'd definitely overheard Nurse Charles in Theatre, enthusing about her ring. Neil had taken it now, and it was at a jewellers in Romsey, being enlarged.

She tried to put it all to the back of her mind as she put on a plastic apron and went into Delivery-Room Four. Her patient, a pretty blonde girl named Sara, was in the process of delivering her first baby. She had now reached the second stage and was ready to start the hard work of pushing.

As Pippa entered, Sister Foster was listening to the foetal heart. She straightened up and gave Pippa a rare smile.

'She's doing fine, Nurse Garland,' she said smoothly. 'But I don't think you'll be capable of doing the delivery.'

'Why ever not?' Was it going to be a forceps delivery?

'Put on some sterile gloves and you'll soon see.

Mystified, Pippa did as she was told.

'I'd like you to check on the position, if you don't mind,' said Annette smoothly. 'See what you think.'

Pippa examined the girl as gently as she could, and her eyes grew wide. Looking at Annette, she said, 'It isn't a normal vertex, it's all lumpy, little bumps and dents, so it can't be a breech . . .'

She took off her gloves. Annette smiled smugly.

'I've sent for Dr Reed,' she said. 'It's a face presentation. So I think he ought to deal with it, don't you?'

Pippa felt indignant. 'But I'm sure it felt like a mento-anterior,' she argued. 'The chin was uppermost, I'm sure. So it should be possible to deliver it normally. I read in my textbook—'

'Reading isn't doing,' said Annette, flushing darkly. 'It's Sara's first baby, and we can't risk anything happening just because it's your first face presentation. I suppose I ought to deliver it myself, but I think Dr Reed—ah, here he is now.'

Pippa deliberately kept her gaze averted as Julian strode into the room. She could feel his eyes on her, but she pretended to be timing Sara's pulse.

'What's wrong?' he asked Sister Foster.

Annette fluttered her eyelashes, and looked up at him with her big brown eyes. 'Nothing wrong, Julian.' He lowered his eyebrows. 'It's a face presentation.'

'Mento-posterior?'

Annette hesitated. 'Anterior.'

'I'm sure you can cope with that, Sister Foster,' he said sharply, and turned to go. 'It is deliverable, I'm sure.'

'Actually, this was meant to be Nurse Garland's case, but she isn't qualified yet, she's only read it in a book, and it is Sara's first baby. We don't want to put her off having any more, do we? After all, there could be minor complications.'

'I don't see why there should be. Is it a very large baby? Small mother?' He crossed to the bed and made a deft examination. Sara took a gulp of gas and oxygen through a mask. Julian patted her arm and smiled.

'I can't imagine there'll be any problems,' he said, and turned to Annette. 'I shall be around if you want me.'

90

'I'm not very happy about it—'

'OK, if you're so worried I'll stay here while Nurse Garland delivers it. She needs the experience of abnormal presentations. Although you don't really need me here, Sister.'

Annette bit her lip. 'I'm very grateful—' she began.

'You've had years of experience,' he said, and pulled on a mask. Over it, his deep blue eyes surveyed Pippa as she donned her sterile green gown and gloves. Before Annette could step forward to tie the tapes on her gown, Julian was already there, and Pippa felt his fingers softly moving against her neck.

Sara was pushing hard, and the baby's face was becoming visible. It was not a common situation, but if the chin was uppermost, the baby could usually be born normally.

'It's quite simple, Nurse Garland,' Julian was saying, as the face appeared yet again. 'As long as you remember to flex the head instead of extending it. The membranes are still intact, so puncture them quickly—come on, before it recedes again—'

Pippa fumbled on the trolley for a suitable instrument, but even as she picked up the forceps, the face had slipped back.

'You're too slow,' Julian accused her. Pippa knew her hands were trembling, and that wouldn't do. She had to keep her control. She glanced at Annette Foster. She had thought

91

the sister might have defended her, but she was quiet, occasionally glancing at Julian over the top of her mask.

'She's going to need an episiotomy,' said Julian. 'Had you realised that? It's a larger diameter to be delivered. Now get those membranes punctured. Right—do it now—this second—'

As the little face appeared yet again, Pippa tried her hardest to pierce the transparent membrane which covered it. Gosh, she'd never realised how tough it was. The contraction was going, she had to do it now . . . Frantically, she pinched the membrane again. Scissors would be better, but they could be dangerous so near to the baby eyes. Ah—she'd made a hole. The fluid gushed out. The contraction had passed, and the baby's head had slipped back very slightly.

'Next contraction it will crown,' said Julian sharply. 'So give the local anaesthetic now.'

Flustered at his tone, Pippa reached blindly for the prepared syringe, and knocked over a gallipot of antiseptic. She heard tutting sounds from Julian, and flushed. She couldn't look at him. She quickly gave Sara the local anaesthetic, and picked up the sterile scissors, waiting to the next contraction to push the baby's head out. Sara took a deep breath and began to push. Quickly, Pippa made the small cut in the perineum, and began to ease out the head. It seemed strange, flexing the head towards the chest, instead of extending it. The head slowly slipped out, as Sara obediently panted. She lay back against the pillows.

'Is it nearly over?' she asked.

'You're doing fine,' said Pippa encouragingly. 'The head is born. One more push will do it.' She realised she'd said the wrong thing when Annette sniffed.

'You won't need to push,' the sister corrected her. 'The contraction will push it out.'

She glanced at Pippa, but the pupil was busy wiping the baby's eyes, and checking that the cord wasn't—oh, hell, it was! It was round the baby's neck! She could feel it, a thick soft rope. She tried to lift it over the baby's face, but it was too tight—no, there were two coils . . .

Her look of distress must have showed.

'What's wrong, Nurse Garland?' asked Julian sharply. Why was he so angry with her? What had she done?

'The cord's round the neck. Twice. I can't lift it over—'

'Then clamp and cut it. Now! Before the next contraction. Come on, you haven't got time to dither.'

Her eyes smarted as she almost said, I'm not dithering. But she tightened her mouth, grabbed the two pairs of small forceps and clamped the cord, leaving a few inches between. Even as she tried to insert the special cord scissors, she could feel the next contraction, pushing the baby's body against her fingers.

'Don't push, Sara! Pant!' she called out, feeling she was fighting a losing battle. Ah— got it— Even as she cut, the baby's body was rotating and pushing against the other loop of cord. But now it was cut it was simple to lift that other loop over the baby's head. Almost crying with relief, she gently lifted out the baby and laid it on the towel. Immediately, it took a deep breath, its little face reddened, and it cried. A wide smile spread across Sara's face.

'What is it?' she asked.

'A girl,' said Pippa, suddenly aware that her hands were shaking. Thankfully, it was soon all over without further complications.

'I'll stay and suture,' said Julian. 'If you'll give me the needle and thread.'

Pippa was all fingers and thumbs, knocking a packet of catgut to the floor as she laid out what he wanted. He looked crossly at her.

'Sister Foster, will you help, please? Nurse Garland is a walking disaster area.' His tone was so curt, tears came to Pippa's eyes. Didn't he realise it was all because of him that she was a disaster area? Any other doctor wouldn't have this effect on her. Neil never had . . .

She went to weigh the baby and measure it, and check it had nothing wrong. Julian finished suturing, and pushed the used trolley towards her without speaking.

'Cup of tea, Julian?' asked Sister Foster

softly. He smiled at her.

'Thanks very much. I'd love one.'

They left together, and Pippa started the task of clearing up the mess, and making sure Sara was all right. In the utility-room, clearing the trolley, all she could remember was his curt tone, and the way he'd tutted at her in front of Annette Foster. How the sister must have enjoyed her discomfiture. Why she disliked Pippa so much, she didn't know.

Well, he'd gone back to the office with her, and they'd sit and drink tea together, and Annette would flutter her eyelashes at him.

It wasn't fair! She hated him! Hated him! Angry frustrated tears ran down her cheeks as she threw green towels and gowns into a skip. Behind her, the door swung open. Sister Foster, no doubt, come to gloat and find fault. Surprising, though, that she could tear herself away from Julian Reed. Perhaps she'd forgotten something. She'd blame Pippa.

Pippa sniffed back the angry tears, and wiped her face with a gauze swab.

'Oh, dear, dear, we can't have this, can we?' The soft velvet voice made her heart lurch. She dropped a pair of forceps and stiffened. He gently grasped her arms and turned her to face him. He reached out, and a finger traced the path of a tear. For a brief, heart-stopping moment his gaze was on her trembling mouth. She unconsciously lifted her face for his kiss.

'I'm sorry, Pippa,' he said. 'I shouldn't have

taken out my bad temper on you. You really did very well with that difficult delivery.'

'You could have fooled me,' she said bitterly.

'I know. I came to apologise. I don't know what makes me do it to you. Unless it's your gorgeous red hair.'

'My red hair again,' she said furiously. 'You certainly have a thing about red hair. Well, I can't help it if I look like Olivia—'

Too late, she realised she'd said the wrong thing. But it couldn't have been a secret. Stella had told her. And he had called her Olivia himself.

His hands dropped from her arms. A muscle twitched in his cheek.

'What do you know about Olivia?' he demanded. 'You're nothing like Olivia! Olivia wouldn't stand there snivelling like that after I'd told her off. She'd have got up and—' He stopped, his mouth tightened.

'And gone?' finished Pippa quietly. 'She couldn't have loved you.' She knew the words were hurting him, but she couldn't help it. She had to hurt him as he had hurt her.

His blue eyes were dark, the pupils large. He stared at her, moved closer.

'What do you know about Olivia?' he repeated in a dangerously calm voice.

'Nothing—Stella—she didn't really tell me anything about her—except to say I look like her. And you were engaged to her. I don't

96

know why she told me anything in the first place—'

'I don't want you to mention Olivia again. Understood? It's in the past. Forgotten.'

She nodded, her green eyes big and dark.

'And I shall make sure you don't talk about her,' he said harshly, and pulled her towards him. At first, she tried to push him away, but then his lips came down on hers, angry and hard. They seemed to search her own lips, seeking a response. The earthquake inside Pippa seemed to grow until she felt like bursting, her heart was thudding like a sledgehammer, her ears were singing, and she didn't really want to struggle at all . . .

Her arms crept around his neck, and as they did so he suddenly thrust her away. His blue eyes were glittering. Just like lapis lazuli. Pippa's knees felt weak and trembly. She'd wanted him to kiss her, but she'd never imagined it would be like that.

'There! Perhaps that will keep you quiet!' Without glancing back, he strode out of the little room. Pippa was unable to move. Her mouth felt bruised by the pressure of his lips, and her heart just would not slow down. She felt like shouting it from the rooftops—He has kissed me! But, of course, she couldn't tell anyone. And he knew this. There was Neil to consider. Kind, gentle Neil.

Calm, and outwardly serene, she carried on with her job. The baby began to cry. Smiling,

Pippa went out to Sara and gave her the baby to hold. All was tidy. All was well. Yes, of course all was well. She'd go and make Sara a nice cup of tea.

*   *   *

'Neil came up to Ward Six today,' said Lucy, when they met at lunch.

'Did he? What for?'

'You'll never believe it, but we have a Chilean girl on the ward, married to an Englishman. She's very pretty, but she speaks very little English yet. I—I saw Neil, so I asked him to help. He and Paola had quite a long chat. She was over the moon when he left. You'll have to watch him, Pippa, all the patients are quite smitten by him, and wanted to know why he'd hidden himself away in South America.'

Pippa laughed. She could never be jealous of the patients. They all fell in love with their doctors. She wasn't really jealous of anyone. And Lucy would have . . .

'You told them he was engaged, I suppose?'

'Well, no, the opportunity never arose. It doesn't matter. He was very charming to them, but they didn't need to know that he's in love with you. Another coffee?'

'No, thank you.'

'Well, I have to be back. We're hectic.' Lucy stood up and straightened her skirt. 'Do you

98

see much of Dr Reed?'

Pippa felt a tell-tale flush creep up her face. 'Now and again, naturally. He does most of the instrumentals.'

'Sounds like an orchestra!' laughed Lucy. 'Talking of which, Annette Foster seems to be playing his tune.'

'What do you mean?'

'You must have seen them together. She works with you.'

'I know she's been playing up to him, but she always does,' said Pippa.

'Yes, well, Julian Reed seems to like it. I can't tell you what I saw—no, I can't—and anyway, a kiss means nothing these days. And how could you be interested?'

'I'm not interested.' Pippa spoke sharply. 'And I didn't know you went in for gossip, Lucy.'

'Ah! "The lady doth protest too much methinks." Or words of that ilk. Shakespeare, wasn't it? He knew a thing or two. Perhaps Neil should know a thing or two.'

'Don't be silly, Lucy.'

'Let me finish my quote. "The brightness of the eye, the pinkness of the cheek—"'

'That's not Shakespeare.'

'No, that's original Lucy Waters. But you're quite right. Why should you be interested when you have the luscious Neil?'

She smiled brightly and hurried away. Pippa dawdled over her coffee, wondering. Was it obvious, the way his name affected her? She'd have to control it. But as long as Neil didn't hear any rumours, she'd be all right. After all, there was no truth in them.

She put down her cup, determined no one would find her running after the arrogant, womanising Julian Reed!

*   *   *

The afternoon was busy. Pippa was put in charge of a plump diabetic woman having her third baby. She had been induced at thirty-six weeks because of the size of the baby—babies of diabetic mothers tended to be large—and was almost in the second stage when Pippa took over from Jane Marshall who had a half-day.

Although a large baby—it had been estimated at around ten pounds—it would still be classed as premature, and would have to go to SCBU for a while. There weren't any problems, despite its size, and soon, with Pippa's help, a beautiful baby boy lay in Joan Greening's arms. Pippa felt she had coped with the delivery really well, and only afterwards did she suspect it was because Julian Reed hadn't been breathing down her neck. It was becoming obvious to her that his presence was a hindrance rather than a help.

She tucked the baby into the perspex crib and wheeled him out of the room. Sister

100

Brayford was staying with Joan until Pippa came back. As she wheeled the crib along the corridor to the lifts, she caught a glimpse of a tall, white-coated figure ahead of her, leaving the reception area. Her heart gave a jolt until she realised, as he turned, it wasn't Julian, but one of the housemen, Dr Clarke. From the back he had looked similar.

The sight of him caused her to remember the scene in the utility-room, recalling the feel of his lips on hers, and her heart started its familiar lurching. Damn you, Julian Reed! she said to herself. I was happy until you came.

She stepped out of the lift and began to push the crib down the corridor towards SCBU. A group of nurses passed her, heading in the opposite direction, and some smiled at her. Unexpectedly, and quite without foundation, she felt they were laughing at her, they knew what a fool she was making of herself over Julian Reed. If Lucy had noticed, then others had. The thought made her face grow hot.

Come, come, Philippa Garland, she admonished herself. This will never do. Lucy was joking, of course she didn't suspect anything. Forget Julian Reed. You're engaged to Neil who loves you. That man only loves himself. And a girl in his past. Neil wouldn't tease you, humiliate you in front of others, he wouldn't kiss you in anger, as Julian did.

Her mind was confused as she reached

SCBU. She pushed the crib into the reception hall and pressed the bell for attention. Through the glass windows she could see nurses moving about purposefully. She could see the ends of the glass-sided cubicles, where the nurses were feeding the minute scraps of humanity that had been born too soon. Diane's baby would be there. Was he still hanging on to life?

A nurse in protective gown and overshoes came to the door to receive the baby.

'Diabetic mother,' said Pippa, handing her the notes. 'Thirty-six weeks. Normal delivery. Weight ten pounds three ounces. Four point six kilograms.'

The nurse nodded absently, gazing at the written details. Over her shoulder Pippa could see two doctors emerging from a cubicle, talking earnestly. With a shock she realised one of them was Neil. What on earth was he doing here? But, of course, she reasoned, why shouldn't he be here? He was an experienced paediatrician, there was no reason why an old colleague couldn't call on him for advice.

The nurse was still reading the delivery details. Pippa tensed as Neil and the other paediatrician turned towards the door. She couldn't just push the crib to the nurse and say, Sorry, I've got to go. Neil didn't appear to have seen her yet. If only the nurse would hurry . . .

She frowned. Why was she thinking like

this? Neil was her fiancé, she loved him, she was going to marry him. What was she thinking of, anxiously wanting to get away before he saw her?

It was too late. As the nurse took the crib Neil glanced across, and his eyes widened. He said something to the other doctor, who glanced at Pippa too, and smiled. Pippa forced a smile to her face. She'd have to make some excuse . . .

They pulled off their cotton overshoes and came into the reception hall.

'I didn't think I'd get to see you, Pippa,' said Neil, his grey eyes crinkling with pleasure.

'Yes, it's nice, Neil, but I'm really rather busy—' She turned to leave, but he grasped her arm.

'I was telling John about you,' said Neil proudly.

'So you're finally tying the knot,' said John Crossland.

'January the eleventh. Isn't that so, Pippa?' He still held her arm possessively.

'Then you're going back to Chile together?' asked John.

'For another two years. There's a job waiting for Pippa. They're very short of well-qualified midwives.'

'What an opportunity for you, Pippa,' enthused John Crossland. 'A chance to see the world.'

'There are more places in the world than

Chile,' said Pippa with asperity. John raised his eyebrows. Neil frowned.

'Yes, it will be a great opportunity,' she said quickly, anxious to get away before any more of her life was mapped out for her. Two children, would it be? Or four? Perhaps Neil hadn't decided for her yet. And a home in London? Or did Neil prefer the provinces?

'I can only wish you all the best,' said John sincerely, and kissed her on the cheek. 'Must dash now. Got to see a baby on the Isolation Ward.' He hurried away, and Pippa turned to follow.

'You seem in a terrible hurry,' said Neil, looking into her eyes.

She looked away. 'Yes, I am. It's been nice seeing you—'

'That makes us sound like strangers,' said Neil, trying to make a joke of it. But his eyes were serious, troubled.

'Don't be silly, Neil.'

'You let John kiss you. What about me? Don't I get one before you run away and leave me?'

Pippa gave a little shiver. 'I just happen to be on duty, Neil. I'm not running away.'

He drew her close, and placed his lips on hers. She found herself tensing instead of responding. What was the matter with her? She opened her eyes, and over Neil's shoulder she could see a doctor and Sister James leaving a cubicle. The doctor—oh, God!—it was Julian—and he was coming this way!

She gently removed herself from Neil's embrace, her thoughts in turmoil. It was so embarrassing, being found like this. And by Julian of all people. Her heart was pounding, but not with passion. And it was in that moment she realised she wasn't in love with Neil, she'd never been in love with him. And she couldn't possibly marry him.

CHAPTER SEVEN

Pippa knew she had to leave before Julian reached the reception hall.

'I really have to go, Neil,' she said shakily.

'I'll pick you up at seven tomorrow,' said Neil.

'Yes. All right.'

'We'll have a meal somewhere?'

'Oh—I'm not sure—I must go.' Out of the corner of her eye she could see Julian taking his leave of Sister James. She pulled open the door and almost ran in to the short corridor which led to the main one. The long corridor was empty. She stood for a moment, her back to the wall, breathing hard. She felt she'd run a mile. Emotion, she decided. And shock. Yet was it such a shock to discover she wasn't in love with Neil after all? Hadn't she felt reluctant to commit herself ever since he'd come back?

She tightened her lips. Her mother had talked her into this; perhaps she'd like to get her out of it!

She heard footsteps in the short corridor, coming from SCBU. If it were Julian, she couldn't let him find her here, emotional and upset. He'd only say, I told you so. She'd never forget the way he'd looked at her, across Neil's shoulder, the sardonic curl to his lip. She'd never seen him look like that before.

She hurried along the corridor, glad when some people emerged from X-ray, and Julian—if it was Julian behind her—couldn't call out to her.

When she arrived back at the Delivery Suite, she found Sister Brayford writing up the notes, and the room was all spick and span. Joan Greening was talking happily about her plans for the new baby, and how excited her other children would be to have a little brother.

Sister turned as Pippa entered, and her shrewd glance took in the girl's flushed complexion.

'Been running, Nurse Garland?'

'Hurrying. I—I met someone who held me up for a while.'

Sister Brayford didn't comment. 'We're nearly finished here,' she told Pippa. 'Check Mrs Greening's TPR and blood-pressure, and if she's all right she can have a cup of tea. I'm

106

sure you'd like that, wouldn't you, dear?'

Joan Greening made herself more comfortable on the hard delivery table.

'I'd love one. And can my hubby have one? He went to phone my mother.'

'Of course he can. I'll send him back to you.'

'He's probably having a cigarette in the waiting-room,' laughed Joan. 'He'd given them up until today!'

'The notes are complete, Sister Garland,' said Sister. 'You know where she's got to go, of course.'

Pippa stared at her. Her recent shock of revelation seemed to have dented her faculties. Had Sister told her? She didn't recall her saying anything about the ward. Her blank expression made Sister frown.

'Ward Three, of course,' she said sharply. 'She's diabetic.'

'Oh, yes, of course.'

Sister gave her a sharp look and left the room. Pippa was feeling confused. She kept recalling Neil's last kiss, and her instinctive resistance. She'd have to tell him. She couldn't let him go on thinking she was going to marry him. So it would have to be the next time she saw him. Tomorrow night. This evening he was taking his mother to visit an old friend. But it would have to be before the arrangements for the Friday party were really under way. Could he have already invited people? Lots of people knew of the engagement; he'd told all his ex-colleagues. Oh, well, he'd just have to tell them it was off. Make some excuse.

She began to feel guilty. No one liked to admit they'd been jilted. Poor Neil. What would he tell them? And what would he tell his parents? And Pippa's mother—she was expecting them to visit tomorrow afternoon. She'd put off important plans of her own in order to see them. No doubt she'd be wanting to discuss arrangements for the wedding.

Pippa felt as though she had a heavy weight inside her. It would be so much easier just to let things slide, let them go on as before, not tell Neil how she felt. But she knew she'd only regret it. She made a tight smile as she popped a thermometer in Joan Greening's mouth, and started to count her pulse.

She'd tell Neil tomorrow night as soon as she saw him. There was no point in putting it off. She'd tell him it was all over.

Joan Greening was watching her. Holding the thermometer in her mouth with the other hand, she said softly, 'You won't forget I don't have sugar in my tea, will you?'

That evening Pippa spent her time busily cleaning the flat, anything to take her mind off what was to come. Lucy was on duty until nine, but by then Pippa was tucked up in bed with a book. She didn't feel like talking to her friend at the moment. Lucy would be bound to talk about Neil, and Pippa felt she couldn't face that just yet. Not until after the deed was done.

She had a sleepless night, worrying about Neil's reaction. Next morning, Lucy remarked on how quiet she was. Pippa immediately made an effort to talk lightly about unimportant things, but it was obvious Lucy wasn't deceived.

'I expect it's the excitement,' she said. 'Anticlimax and all that. It isn't every day one gets engaged.'

Her voice was brittle, her eyes bright. Pippa suspected trouble with the boyfriend in London. She wished she'd tell her about it. But perhaps she was feeling like Pippa, trying to keep it below the surface.

It was soon time to go on duty, so they separated. The morning on Delivery Suite was quiet. Pippa delivered a baby boy just before lunch, and took the mother and baby up to Ward Six. Lucy was too busy to talk; she seemed cross and irritable and Pippa was glad to leave. She got into the lift and went down to the dining-room.

When she returned to the Delivery Suite at half-past one, she was sent to take over from Jane Marshall in Labour-Room Seven. But before she could do so, Sister Brayford drew her aside.

'Mrs Jordan isn't to be left for one moment,' she said in a low voice. Pippa held her breath. Another eclampsia? No, she'd be in a delivery-room.

'Nurse Marshall won't be able to tell you

about her, not in front of her, so I'll tell you now. Gwen Jordan is a schizophrenic.'

'Uncontrolled?' asked Pippa. She'd spent eight weeks of her general training in a psychiatric hospital, so she'd met a few schizophrenics. The worst ones were difficult to control, extremely unpredictable. Many were treated successfully, and were able to live normal lives in the community. But a pregnant schizophrenic posed lots of problems—for nurse, mother, and baby.

'As you know, pregnancy causes stress in some mothers. Even controlled schizophrenics are liable to relapse under stress.' She watched Pippa's reaction.

'Mrs Jordan has relapsed?'

Sister nodded. 'Until a few weeks ago she had managed without taking any drugs for over a year. When she told her doctor she was pregnant, he saw no reason to terminate it unless she got too bad.'

'And, I suppose,' said Pippa, 'by the time she did relapse it was too late to terminate.'

'She was thirty-five weeks. She's not really too bad, quite amenable to suggestion, you should have no trouble doing recordings. She's on a low dose of haloperidol which seems to be keeping her fairly stable. So far, that is. The risk increases as she approaches the second stage. We just don't know how she'll react.'

'Is her husband with her?' asked Pippa.

Sister Brayford gave a rueful smile.

'Unfortunately, he dashed off to the dentist about an hour ago. Said he had raging toothache. Perhaps it was just an excuse. I don't know. I doubt if he'll come back before the delivery.'

'How far on is she?'

'She shouldn't be more than an hour or two. We've given her pethidine, but we daren't give her too much because of the strong tranquillisers she's on.'

Pippa nodded, understanding.

'Although she seems to be behaving quite well, we mustn't forget she is mentally ill,' said Sister. 'She is not to be left for a second.'

'Of course.'

'Ring the bell if you need anyone.'

Wondering how it was she always seemed to get the difficult cases, Pippa went across to Room Seven and opened the door. Jane Marshall, a few months junior to Pippa, was writing on the chart. She turned and grinned at Pippa.

'So I can have my lunch at last!' she exclaimed. 'I'm absolutely starving!' Pippa smiled and glanced at the patient.

Gwen Jordan had long fair hair, some of it caught up in a red bow on top of her head. She had a narrow pointed face, and big hazel eyes. Pippa found it difficult to believe she was mentally ill—she looked so calm and serene as she watched the two midwives.

'Do you know about Gwen?' asked Jane

anxiously.

'Yes, Sister's given me the gen.'

Jane looked relieved. 'I'll leave you then. I've got a half-day. Going to Kew Gardens with Phil.' She turned to Gwen. 'Bye, Gwen. I hope you have what you want.'

'A boy,' said Gwen, twiddling her hair. 'His name is Peter, but she didn't choose. She isn't allowed.'

'Never mind,' said Jane cheerfully. She winked at Pippa and left. Pippa read the last recordings on the chart. Everything seemed fine. She could sense Gwen watching her, so she turned and smiled encouragingly at her. 'How are you feeling, Gwen? Are you well?' Such a silly question, she thought. It merited a silly answer.

'Well? Well?' echoed Gwen. 'Ding dong bell, pussy's in the well. Well, well. What a lot of wells. Do you want me to tell you?'

'I'd just like to know how you are. Are the contractions strong?'

'She's not going to tell you anything, you know.' She clamped her mouth shut and started to hum.

Mystified, Pippa turned back to the charts. She noticed that Derek, the husband, was listed as next of kin.

'Is Derek pleased about the baby, Gwen?'

'Yes, she is called Gwen. He is called Derek. Have you met Peter?'

'Peter? I thought you were calling the baby

Peter, if it's a boy. I can't meet him until he's born, Gwen.'

Sounded logical, thought Pippa. But Gwen's logic was different from normal people's.

'Silly. Of course you can meet him. That's what they use. That!' She gestured towards the foetal stethoscope. Pippa laughed with relief.

'Oh, that! Yes, I can hear the baby's heartbeat with that. Would you like me to listen?'

'If you like. She's not bothered.'

Gwen was due for more recordings, and Pippa felt she was in the right mood to co-operate, so she picked up the Pinard's stethoscope. Gwen obligingly held her yellow cotton nightdress aside so she could listen. It was fine. As Pippa straightened up Gwen said, 'What did he tell you?'

'It's only his heartbeat, Gwen.'

'He talks! He talks to me! The other nurse told me what she'd heard.'

'Oh. And what did he say to her?'

Gwen was not fooled. She looked slyly at Pippa. 'Just words. What words did he say this time?'

'Well, he seemed to be saying it won't be long now before you can see him as well as hear him.'

Gwen's eyes narrowed. 'He said that last time! Hasn't he got any imagination?'

Perhaps I haven't got any imagination, thought Pippa. And supposing the baby was a girl? Would she still call it Peter? While Gwen was feeling so helpful, Pippa took the opportunity of taking her blood-pressure. Gwen watched the procedure with interest. When it was done she said, 'She always wanted to be a nurse. She played at Doctors and Nurses.'

Pippa suddenly realised Gwen was talking about herself.

'Why didn't she become a nurse?'

'Her mother said no, no, no. Her mother said she wasn't clever enough.'

'Isn't she clever?'

Gwen laughed. 'Cleverer than you!'

Pippa didn't doubt that. She wrote the recordings on the chart, then went and sat on a chair by the window. Gwen suddenly sat bolt upright in bed and looked at her. She cleared her throat as if to start a speech.

'Did you know,' she began, in a conversational tone, 'did you know that the momentous foetal displacement in a uterine body, with, of course, all the aqueous transmission of electricity surrounding the viscous circumference, can cause positive contractions of the polarity?'

Pippa stared for a moment, open-mouthed. It sounded like sense, yet at the same time it didn't. She swallowed, and nodded.

'That's very interesting, Gwen. Very interesting.' Gwen smiled and lay down again. Occasionally, her hand rested on her stomach, and she grimaced. Pippa sensed she was beginning to feel the contractions again. But it was too late to give her more pethidine.

Pippa gazed out of the window. From the bed came a low muttering. She glanced round, and Gwen gave her a vacuous smile.

'Such a preponderance of butterflies.'

'Butterflies?'

'Butterflies in there.' She patted her stomach. 'When they're ready I shall set them free, to fly away.'

Well, someone's in for a shock, thought Pippa. As far as she knew, babies didn't fly. And it crossed her mind that someone was going to have to look after the baby, because, in her present state, Gwen certainly couldn't.

Gwen started to mumble again, louder. Like an incantation. Occasionally she gave a little grunt, and Pippa suspected she was almost in the second stage. It was time someone came to look at her.

'Butterflies, butterflies, cats and dogs, pigs and hogs, coal and logs, toads and frogs—' She laughed, then caught her breath and moaned. Pippa decided to ring the bell for assistance. The flex of the bell-push hung from the wall. The bell at the end of it was tucked firmly under the pile of pillows. Casually she reached out to take it, and Gwen's hand shot out and grasped her arm. Her grip was like steel.

'Go away, go away, go away!'

There was only one thing for it. She would

have to go to the door to attract attention. Nonchalantly, she moved past the end of the bed.

'I'll get you a drink, Gwen,' she said in a loud voice. Gwen took no notice and continued her bizarre rhymes.

'Shoes and clogs, bigs and bogs—' She hesitated, grunted, and began a new rhyme. 'Butterflies, ears and eyes, lives and dies, clouds and skies—'

She was really quite clever, thought Pippa, moving casually towards the door and opening it. Quite imaginative rhymes. She peered out. The nurses' station was deserted. Behind her, the rhyming had stopped, and a low moaning had begun. Please, someone, come! She stepped just outside, willing someone to come her way. But all was quiet. She could hear quick footsteps some way away, too far away to help her. She turned back—as Gwen grabbed a pair of scissors from her handbag and held them menacingly over her swollen abdomen.

'No—Gwen—no!'

With speed she didn't know she had in her, Pippa launched herself at the bed and grabbed Gwen's arm. Gwen began to scream and thrash about, trying to prise Pippa's fingers from her wrist. She was very, very strong, and Pippa doubted she could hold on for long. If only she could reach the bell-push, but it was on the other side of the bed, right under the pillow, and Gwen was so violent there was no chance of reaching it.

She increased her pressure on the girl's arm, hoping to make her drop the scissors. She temporarily forgot to watch her other arm, and a sudden blow on her left cheekbone made her gasp and almost lose her grip. But the life of a baby was at stake. She dared not give in. Her head reeling from the blow, she decided protection of the baby was her first priority. She lay across Gwen's stomach, just as the scissors came down . . .

Gwen's arm suddenly jerked back, and the scissors went flying to the floor. The girl began to scream, but firm hands held her down, and a deep velvet voice said, 'Get the intramuscular haloperidol, Sister.'

In a daze, Pippa moved from the bed, and watched helplessly as Sister Brayford plunged the needle deep into Gwen's thigh. Gwen screamed again, and began to cry. She seemed to relax then, and as Julian's hands released her, she pulled the sheet around her, and curled up in a ball.

Julian stepped back from the bed and looked hard at Pippa.

'Are you hurt?'

'No—not really—'

'Your cheek is red. And your hand is bleeding.' He tilted her chin and gently examined the bruised cheekbone.

'She struck you?' he asked gently, and Pippa felt herself sinking, drowning, in that dark blue gaze.

She nodded. 'It isn't much. And the bleeding, it's only a little nick where the scissors caught me.'

He took her hand and examined the cut. The long slim fingers were strong but gentle.

'It doesn't need stitches,' Pippa said shakily. It was most peculiar—she felt almost grateful to Gwen for injuring her, for making it necessary for this blue-eyed demi-god to touch her and speak to her. And to think she'd tried to avoid him earlier!

The sudden remembrance of what Julian had witnessed in SCBU caused her cheeks to flame. The way he had looked at her then! Yet now—but of course, he was just being professional now. He couldn't just ignore her obvious injuries.

'I'm really fine. I'll just get a plaster for my hand—'

'You'd better go off duty,' said Sister Brayford, keeping an eye on Gwen, now withdrawn and silent.

'No, really, I'm fine. She didn't hurt me.'

Julian moved away to the end of the bed. 'How on earth did she manage to get those scissors?' he asked, crossing to the sink and washing his hands.

'They were in her handbag,' said Pippa, getting a small plaster from the cupboard.

'Then you must have seen her looking in her handbag,' said Sister Brayford.

'No—I—well—' she took a deep breath '—I was feeling a bit worried about her, I was sure she was almost in the second stage, but she was talking funny, making rhymes, and she stopped me using the bell, so I had to come to the door to see if anyone—'

'You left her unattended?' Julian was aghast.

'No, not unattended. I just stood in the doorway—looking for someone—' Why was he looking at her like that?

'With your back to her?' He sounded stern.

'Yes,' she said in a small voice.

'You realise she could have damaged her baby?' His voice was quiet, but full of authority.

'I didn't think—I do now—I'm sorry—'

'Never mind, there's been no great disaster,' said Sister Brayford, trying to defuse the situation. 'And they were only nail scissors. You were very brave, Nurse Garland, to tackle her the way you did. You'll have quite a bruise on your face.'

Pippa touched it tentatively. It did feel sore.

'I'll check to see if she really is in the second stage,' said Julian curtly. 'She's doing a bit of grunting.'

Pippa watched in dumb misery as Sister Brayford efficiently coaxed Gwen into the correct position for the examination. Soon it was over, and Julian peeled off his gloves.

'Wheel her round to delivery. She'll be no

119

good at pushing, I doubt if she'll co-operate, so I'll do a forceps. Bring the gas and oxygen, Nurse Garland.' He didn't even glance at her, and Pippa knew he was disappointed in her. She had made a big mistake, and she had failed.

She said nothing as she wheeled the anaesthetic trolley round to the delivery-room behind Sister Brayford and the bed.

'I'll do a pudendal nerve block,' said Julian, once Gwen was safely in position on the table, her feet in lithotomy stirrups. 'And get me the Barnes Neville forceps, please.'

He scrubbed up, and donned his green gown and sterile gloves.

'Well—tie him up, Nurse Garland,' said Sister briskly, as she checked the trolley packs.

Her hands shaking, Pippa took the top tapes, acutely aware of the soft skin of his neck, and the way his dark hair curled into the nape. She had an irresistible urge to stroke it. Quickly, she tied all the tapes and stepped back. Julian seated himself and began.

Pippa felt she would never tire of watching him work; the way his long surgeon's fingers moved skilfully yet gently, injecting the nerve block, inserting the blades of the forceps, and gently but firmly pulling the baby out into the world.

At one point he must have sensed her intense gaze, for he looked up and his blue eyes met hers. Just for an instant. Had she imagined the slight frown? She knew she had really disappointed him, and he would never forget. Neither would she.

On the table, Gwen moaned and moved restlessly, and Sister Brayford, waiting to give the syntometrine as the baby was born, spoke reassuringly to her in a low voice. Pippa felt superfluous. Gwen had rejected the gas and oxygen, so there was nothing for her to do.

'Here he is,' announced Julian, as he carefully withdrew the small vulnerable body. And it was a boy, too. Peter.

'It is a boy,' said Pippa, surprised.

'Didn't I say it was?' said Julian, as he cut the cord, and he didn't sound quite so cross. Perhaps one day he'd forgive her her lapse of concentration.

'It's a boy, Gwen,' said Sister loudly, after giving the injection to help the expulsion of the placenta. Gwen opened her eyes. She seemed confused.

'A boy? Derek?'

'He's not here, but he's coming soon,' said Sister. 'Now you just rest.'

'It was hard work,' said Gwen plaintively, closing her eyes. Sister and Pippa exchanged amused glances. Hard work, when she hadn't contributed one small push.

But it was all over now, and she did seem to be calmer. The third stage was carried out without problems. Julian did the suturing, and he didn't even glance at Pippa as she went

121

about her duties with the baby. Gwen had fallen asleep, so they wisely refrained from letting her hold the baby. Pippa was relieved at this; it was quite on the cards for Gwen to expect the baby to fly away, like a butterfly!

Julian took the notes and left, speaking briefly to Sister Brayford, but ignoring Pippa. After he'd gone, she felt like bursting into tears. Why had he put all the blame on to her? But she was determined not to let his bad temper affect her. He was hateful! How could she have let herself fall under his spell when he was examining her battle scars? He had seemed so sympathetic, then he had turned round and blamed her for it all. It was obvious now that he merely tolerated her, because of her red hair, but that toleration had snapped when she neglected to watch Gwen and almost caused a disaster. Yes, it had been her fault, but she wasn't a psychiatric nurse, how could she know Gwen would suddenly turn violent?

She gritted her teeth as she made tea for Gwen, and her husband, who had just returned minus a tooth. Soon they were all despatched to Ward Two to recover. Sister Brayford turned to Pippa with a smile.

'A difficult case, Nurse Garland,' she said. 'But I think we coped extremely well.'

She was being so kind, thought Pippa, and it made her want to cry again. She wasn't condemning her, as Julian had. She knew what problems nurses had to face. She gave a shaky smile.

'Do you think so, Sister?'

'And you've had a nasty experience. You'll have a lovely bruise there tomorrow. I could send you back to the labour wards, but it's gone three o'clock, so I'm sending you off duty now instead of at five. Go home and rest.'

'Thank you, Sister.' It was true, the experience had shaken her. But what had come to the forefront of her mind now, and was bothering her even more, was the fact that she had to tell Neil tonight that the engagement was off. How would hc take it?

She collected her cloak and went back to her flat. Lucy had a split shift. She was sitting in the kitchen, gazing out of the window, when Pippa arrived. She turned, surprised.

'You're early.' Had she been crying? Her eyes seemed bright.

'Had a difficult case, a schizophrenic—'

'Your face! What happened?'

Pippa sat down and told her, and Lucy made a cup of tea, and Julian's annoyance faded slightly from her mind. They sat at the kitchen table, and talked about other difficult cases, but the conversation was shallow and light. Each one knew the other had something on her mind, but couldn't, or wouldn't, divulge it.

At ten to five, Lucy went on duty, and Pippa sat for a while longer, feeling dissatisfied with herself. She felt hungry, so she made herself an egg on toast. Not too much, because Neil was taking her out for a meal. She bit her lip. She couldn't let him. It would be deceitful of her to allow him to spend money on her before she'd told him what was on her mind. She'd tell him here, in the flat, as soon as he arrived. And she was dreading it.

At five minutes to seven the doorbell rang. Pippa's palms were damp. She wiped them on her skirt as she went along to answer it.

Neil was wearing fawn trousers with a casual cotton jacket over a pale green shirt. His smile faded slightly as his gaze took in her white uniform dress and flat shoes.

'But you're not ready,' he accused, coming inside and giving her a perfunctory peck on the cheek. Pippa was relieved it hadn't been a more passionate kiss. But then, Neil wasn't really an ardent sort of person.

'No—I haven't changed—I don't really want to go out for a meal. I've had a difficult day.'

'What have you done to your face? Walked into a door?'

'A patient's fist.' She explained briefly, anxious to get it all over and done with. She sat down in the sitting-room.

'You'll feel better for going out,' asserted Neil, still standing, obviously not giving in easily. 'And a bit of make-up will cover the bruise, if that's bothering you.'

'No, it isn't that.' Oh, God, this was going to be difficult. 'Please sit down, Neil. I have something to tell you.'

He frowned, and perched himself on the arm of a chair.

'I expect you're cross with me for kissing you in SCBU, aren't you? I sensed you weren't very pleased.'

'Well—yes—but it's not just that. Well, that helped, I suppose, to make me realise—'

'Pippa, you're not making sense.' He sounded cross. She took a deep breath.

'You'll say this doesn't make sense, either,' she said quickly, before she could change her mind. 'And I suppose it doesn't, really. But I've made up my mind. Neil, I can't marry you.'

CHAPTER EIGHT

In the interminable silence the sitting-room clock ticked. Neil's dazed expression seemed to be frozen. Pippa's heart was beating nineteen to the dozen as she waited for his reaction. She was almost afraid to look at him. His mouth opened and closed a couple of times, then he forced a tight smile to his face.

'You're joking, aren't you, Pippa? You have to be joking.'

'I couldn't joke over something like this. You can't imagine how I hate telling you, but—'

'You hate it? Then why are you doing it?'

'Because it has to be done. Neil, I'm not in love with you.' Her voice was desperate.

'How can you say that? Now, after all the plans have been made? Pippa—' he leaned forward, watching her face '—you've always said you loved me. Were you lying?'

'No, Neil. I do love you. In a way.'

He stood then and looked down at her, and she felt impotent and vulnerable as she looked up into his hurt and puzzled face. Still seated, she felt distinctly at a disadvantage, so she stood and faced him.

'In a way?' he echoed. His eyes seemed suddenly cold.

'Yes, like a dear friend. Or a brother. And that isn't a basis for marriage. Surely you wouldn't want me to marry you, knowing I feel like this?'

'There's someone else.' His voice was flat and hard.

'No, Neil, there isn't anyone else. I'm very fond of you, and that's why I can't marry you. I can't ruin your life as well as mine.'

He took off his glasses and wiped them with his handkerchief. Without them, he too looked vulnerable.

Pippa had to fight against the urge to put her arms around him—to say she was sorry, she didn't mean it. He put on his glasses again. They made his eyes seem hard and cold.

'Pippa.' He made a movement as if to hold her, then his hands dropped to his sides. 'I love

126

you, Pippa. Doesn't that mean anything to you?'

Pippa bit her lip. This was a nightmare. 'Of course it does. I shall always value—your friendship.'

He gave a short laugh. 'My friendship? So that's what you think I've been offering all these months! Pippa, how could you?'

His voice was throbbing with emotion. She'd never heard him speak like this before. But it was too late now.

'I'm sorry, Neil. It's better I tell you now, before we've made commitments to each other.'

'But I have made a commitment, Pippa! To you! I gave you a ring.' He grabbed her and pulled her close. She could feel his warmth and strength.

'Neil—' She pulled away.

'Say you've made a mistake, Pippa! Think again. Remember what we had going for us. Work in South America, a big house in Romsey when we come back—'

'A house in Romsey? When did you buy that?'

'I haven't bought one. I'm talking about White Gates. The house is too big for my parents alone, Pippa. We could share it, there's plenty of room, it's a lovely house—'

'I have no intention of living with your parents, Neil! And I've just discovered I don't want to go out to Chile.'

'It's a fine time to discover that,' said Neil in a tight voice. 'When all the arrangements have been made.'

'You had no right to make arrangements for me without asking me first! I suppose you've told your mother we're going to live with them when we come back from Chile?'

'She suggested it, Pippa. I thought it was a good idea.'

'Of course you would. She suggested it because she can't bear to have you out of her sight. She can't let go of the apron strings. Anything your mother suggests is a good idea, isn't it? Was she going to choose my wedding dress?'

Neil's face had a pinched look. His mouth was a narrow line.

'What exactly do you mean by those remarks about my mother?' He spoke through clenched teeth. Pippa should have recognised dangerous ground, but she was too angry to stop now.

'I meant that I've known for a long time, afraid to admit it to myself, and everyone knows, they all say you're a mother's boy, afraid to do anything without her permission. I'm surprised she allowed you to go to Chile!'

One glance at his white face told Pippa she had gone too far. She closed her eyes, waiting for retaliation. But he just seemed too shocked to speak. She touched his arm.

'I'm sorry, Neil—I shouldn't have said—'

'Well, I'm glad you did! Now I know what you're really like! All these months I've been thinking of you as a sweet and kind girl who loved me, who liked my family, but you're just like the rest! My mother saw through them, but she didn't see through you. You're hard, Pippa, you're cruel and deceitful—' His voice broke. 'Oh, Pippa, I had thought you were different—'

His eyes were full of mute appeal. Pippa couldn't stand it any longer. Tears were streaming down her cheeks as she grabbed her jacket from a chair and ran from the flat. It wasn't meant to end like this! Neil should have understood, but he was far too insensitive and self-centred to realise how she was feeling. He hadn't seen how it had hurt her to do it.

Sobbing, she ran down the stairs and through the doors. She didn't know where she was going; she just had to get away from his accusing looks. Gulping back her sobs of anger and frustration, she turned the corner of the building, not even caring where she was going, and bumped, unseeing, into a rock-like figure.

'Sorry—sorry—' She moved aside, her sight blurred by tears, but a strong hand caught her arm.

'Pippa—what's wrong?'

A sob caught in her throat. His deep voice had made her pull up sharp. She couldn't look at him. She couldn't let him see her like this.

'Please let me go!' She tried to prise his

hand from her sleeve.

'Not until you've told me what's wrong.'

'Nothing's wrong. Please let me go!' She swallowed, and made the mistake of looking up into his eyes. They surveyed her compassionately. For a moment she wanted to pour her heart out to him. Then she recalled that time after the Caesarean, when he'd suggested she wasn't in love with Neil. Well, he was right again. But she wasn't going to let him know that!

Still holding her arm he gently wiped her cheek with his long surgeon's fingers, pausing at the bruise just starting to appear.

'Come on,' he said, putting an arm on her shoulder. 'Come and tell uncle all about it.' She giggled weakly. Uncle! She'd never had an uncle quite like Julian Reed. Instinctively, she drew back.

'No. I can't. I can't tell you.'

He considered her face for a moment. 'Fair enough. But I know what will make you feel better.'

Her hand flew to her mouth. 'I've left my flat unlocked! And Neil—'

He gazed at her discerningly. 'Is this an excuse to get out of coming with me?'

'No—oh, it doesn't really matter. I've got nothing worth stealing.'

'Haven't you?' He gave her a strange glance, and she flushed.

'You haven't told me where we're going.'

What was the matter with her? She didn't usually behave so impulsively. He was leading her by the hand towards his cream Rover.

'A little place I know. Hop in.'

She couldn't understand why her knees were trembling as she settled herself into the soft grey upholstery. But they were, and her mouth felt dry.

'But I'm in uniform,' she protested weakly, hugging her beige jacket to her.

He let in the clutch. 'Only partly,' he said. 'And it won't matter.' His hands moved easily on the wheel. Pippa's gaze was drawn towards them. He was wearing navy cords and a white cotton sweater which emphasiscd his tanned skin.

'You don't approve of my driving?' he asked casually as they drove towards the town.

'Oh—yes—you drive very competently.'

'I just wondered, since your gaze seems riveted to the wheel.'

She flushed and turned to look out of the window. 'I'm sorry if I was staring.'

'I have no objection to your staring at me, Pippa.' His voice was light, but Pippa's heart began to thud violently in her chest. She wished he wouldn't tease her. He'd made it patently obvious he had no intention of getting involved with a redhead. So why was he demanding her company? Because he felt sorry for her, that was all. He was kind and well-mannered. It was second nature to him to comfort disturbed nurses. Disturbed anyone, she supposed.

'I'm surprised you want my company after this afternoon,' she said in a small voice, with a sidelong glance.

'What happened this afternoon?' he said innocently. 'Besides a half-mad patient giving you a straight left.'

'How can you say that? You were the one who accused me of negligence, just because I turned my back for a minute.'

'I was? Well, of course, you took a big risk, didn't you? And it could have led to disaster.'

'I know, I know, but she was so deceptive, so calm. She just lay there making up rhymes. And you can't deny I did protect the baby. She hit my hand instead.'

'I was quite aware of that. You were very brave. Sister said so.'

'Then why were you so disapproving? So hostile to me?'

'Was I?' He stopped the car smoothly outside a rather expensive-looking wine bar.

'I could see it in your face, I'd disappointed you. You thought I was a hopeless nurse. I know you don't really like me—'

He switched off the engine and turned to face her. His blue eyes seemed hurt.

'You are too sensitive for your own good,' he said. 'Didn't you stop to think I was angry because you could have been badly hurt?'

Pippa was too amazed to reply. He didn't

seem to expect one, but emptied his long lean body out of the car and came round to open her door. Pippa was still feeling bemused. He was worried that she might get hurt? He cared about her? No, he just felt sorry for her. It couldn't be more than that. He felt sorry for her and that was why he was being so kind. She climbed out of her seat and he locked the door.

The Dionysius Wine Bar was quite new, dimly lit and decorated in the Ancient Greek style; murals of Greek gods, lions, bulls, panthers, and everywhere vine leaves, ivy, and pine cones.

The manager of the bar greetcd Julian in a familiar way, and seemed to know what he liked to drink. Julian joined Pippa at a small table in a corner alcove, and the drinks arrived immediately. Pippa's was a golden colour in a small glass.

'You didn't ask me what I wanted,' she complained. Was this another superior male animal who thought he knew best? Julian grinned at her.

'I promise you'll like it. Taste it.'

It was sweet, with a soft honey flavour. At first she felt it was too sweet, but as she sipped it it seemed to flow through her veins, making her feel warm and relaxed.

'It's nice, whatever it is. You're right, as usual.'

He laughed. 'It's mead. The first

Elizabethans used to drink it.'

'In a Greek wine bar.'

'They make it themselves. And I think I read somewhere once the ancient Greeks drank it, too.'

He sipped his drink, watching her reflectively. She was reluctant to meet his gaze. It made her tremble inside, and the drink was causing her to be in danger of losing her inhibitions.

'Tell me about yourself,' said Julian, leaning back.

'What do you want to know?' Why couldn't they talk about more interesting things, mutual interests, hobbies, books, sports, television? Anything but herself.

He shrugged his shoulders. 'Anything. Everything.'

'You're hoping I'll talk about what happened tonight, aren't you?'

'You've been reading my mind.'

'Then I'll have to disappoint you.'

'Oh? Perhaps another time.'

'There won't be another time.' He was probably already regretting bringing her here.

'You don't like being here with me?' He raised an eyebrow. Pippa felt a thrill run down her spine.

'It's—quite nice.'

'Quite nice?' He raised his hands in mock dismay. Then his expression changed, became serious. 'You're worried what Neil Chappell will say if he hears you've been out with me.'

'No, I'm not! It's nothing to do with him who I—'

She broke off, aware she'd said too much. His gaze was penetrating.

'I suppose you've had a row,' he said flatly. 'Still, it will be even more thrilling when you kiss and make up.'

'Are you speaking from experience?' She twiddled with the stem of her glass.

'Perhaps.'

'Well, I'd rather not talk about him, if you don't mind.'

'I don't mind at all. He's not my type.' Pippa couldn't help laughing, and their eyes met. His gaze was so intense, so blue. She forced her eyes away. 'And I'd much rather talk about you.'

Frantically, she said, 'No, you first.' Then she could keep her own life story to simple details. Julian nodded.

'All right. But I shan't let you off.' The way he said it, almost as a threat, made her shiver.

'I was born in Winchester,' Julian began. 'I went to a good grammar school. Then I became a medical student in London. My mother was a district nurse. She died when I was thirteen. My sister Stella kept house for us until she got married.'

'Is that all? I knew all that. Stella told me.'

'So she did. There's very little more. I'm a very simple, uncomplicated person. My father

135

was a GP. He's retired. He was a good deal older than my mother. I wanted to be a cancer surgeon—my mother had breast cancer—but then Stella had Amy—and you know the rest.'

'Yes,' said Pippa gently, seeing the pain in his eyes. If only he could love her the way he loved that child! But he was still in love with Olivia, and it showed. The way he couldn't even mention her name.

'Yes,' he said tautly. 'It was a tragic business.'

'Isn't there any more? I mean, you must have had friends—'

'Girlfriends, you mean?' His voice had grown harsh. 'No, there were no girlfriends worth mentioning.'

It was obvious he had no intention of telling her about Olivia. And that was a good indication of what she herself meant to him.

'I see.'

'It's your turn now. You promised.'

'Like you, there's not much to tell,' said Pippa lightly. 'I'm an only child, my father was a dentist who walked out on us when I was three. He was killed in a motorway crash three years ago.'

'Touché,' he teased gently. 'I knew that too.'

'My mother and I have always lived in Steep, in the cottage Dad bought for us. My mother—'

'You. Not your mother,' he prompted. She flushed.

136

'I was sent to a private school until I was eighteen. It was very select but they didn't teach us much. I just scraped through enough exams to start nursing training at Kingslake. There's not much to tell, really.'

'No more? No boyfriends?'

'Only Neil.'

'And when do you go out to Chile?' His voice was tight.

'I'm not.' She bit her tongue. She hadn't meant to tell him. But she seemed unable to lie to him, particularly when he looked at her like that, as if he could read her thoughts.

'You're letting him go out to South America without you? That's a strange sort of marriage.'

It was suddenly all too much. 'Please—don't ask me any more—I can't face all these questions!' She put her head on her hands. Then she felt his fingers stroking her hair. She looked up at him, her mouth trembling.

'I'm not marrying him,' she whispered. His hand gently covered hers. The tears fell unchecked down her cheeks.

'You need another drink.' He started to rise.

'No, I'm all right. I'll get over it.'

'Nevertheless, I'm getting you one.' He went to the counter. When he returned Pippa was sniffing and blowing her nose. Instead of sitting opposite, this time Julian came and sat next to her. He smelled nice. She moved fractionally away.

'So it's all over.'

She nodded. 'Go on. Say it. "I told you so".'

'Did you really think I'd say something like that?'

'Well, you're always so damned right!' she burst out, not sure whether she was angry with him or with herself. 'You're too perfect for words!'

'Oh, Pippa, Pippa, I am far from perfect. If I were perfect I wouldn't fall in love with the wrong girls.'

She stared at him. Was he going to tell her about Olivia? Her drink arrived at that moment.

'Drink it up,' he advised her. 'You've had a very traumatic day by the sound of things.'

She nodded and took a sip of the warming liquid.

'It does no good to bottle things up,' he said, and his voice was soft and intimate. 'Now you've told me the engagement's off, why don't you tell me how it happened? You must have loved him once.'

'I still love him. In a way. I confused affection with love,' she said miserably. 'It's all my fault. I suppose I've known him too long. He seems like—a brother to me.'

'Why do you blame yourself? I assume he has faults, too.'

'Oh, yes, he liked to manage me—the "little woman" sort of thing—advise me what I should or shouldn't do. I didn't realise at first.

I thought it was because he cared for me. Then when he came back from Chile, I seemed to see him with clearer eyes, more objectively. And I found I didn't want him planning my life. I wanted to do it myself. I don't want to be tied down yet. I'm only twenty-three.'

'Yes, I know. You're far too young and pretty to bury yourself in South America.'

'You're laughing at me.'

'I'm deadly serious. I can't understand why you agreed to get engaged at all if you felt like that.'

'It was a sort of agreement, a tacit agreement, before he went away. He expected it. And I was feeling confused over my changed feelings, I was unsure of myself. I suppose I let my mother talk me into it. She's always advised me to marry someone steady and reliable. You see, she fell madly in love with my father who was very attractive, and he left her after seven years. She says I shouldn't believe in love at first sight and all that.'

'Don't you believe in love at first sight?' he asked gently, tilting her chin.

'I don't know. I'm too confused.' She could hardly speak, the way he was looking at her. Was he thinking of kissing her again? The idea made her catch her breath.

'Then you've never fallen in love,' he said sadly, releasing her.

'It's probably only infatuation, anyway,' she burst out.

'Because your mother says so? It sounds as if your mother was just plain unlucky in her choice of husband, but she shouldn't assume it's the same for everyone. I know people who have fallen in love and are still very happy after many years of marriage.' He seemed to speak wistfully.

'I wish you'd tell my mother that.'

'Perhaps I will. One day.'

Pippa sipped her mead. This day hadn't turned out a bit as she'd planned. Here she was with a man who both aggravated and attracted her. Even as she wished she were safe and warm in bed, she wanted this evening to go on for ever.

'When did you realise you couldn't marry him?' Julian's soft voice interrupted her thoughts.

'Oh—it wasn't sudden—I just sort of knew.' As she spoke she recalled Neil's kiss in SCBU. Julian nodded. Was he thinking the same?

'I'm not surprised you lacked concentration in your work, with all this on your mind.'

Pippa looked at him indignantly. 'I wasn't lacking in concentration, if it's Gwen you're talking about! I just never imagined she'd become violent like that. Oh, what's the use? You're determined to believe I was totally to blame. I shouldn't have been left in there alone. I'm not psychiatrically trained. Yes, it was my fault. But you don't have to rub it in!'

'I'm sorry. I can see you're still upset. I'll

140

take you home. I hope your flat hasn't been burgled.'

She sat up quickly. 'I hope it isn't locked!'

'But you ran out, you said, leaving it open.'

'Neil was there. I couldn't stand the way he looked at me, the names he called me. God, I felt so guilty! I just ran out without thinking.'

'And you think he may have locked the door behind him when he left?'

Pippa nodded. 'What shall I do if he has?'

'We'll cross that bridge when we come to it,' said Julian, getting up. 'Now I think a good night's sleep is what you need.'

'Is that doctor's orders?'

'If you like.' He glanced at her. 'That bruise is coming out. You'd better tell everyone your ex-fiancé did it, and that's why it's all over.'

Pippa was shocked. 'I couldn't do that! That's a dreadful thing to say! Your idea of a joke, I suppose. Neil is very kind and very gentle—and I've hurt him more than I ever wanted to.'

He slipped her jacket over her shoulders. His face was so near to hers.

'And you are too kind, and too gentle, and far too vulnerable. You need someone to protect you.'

'They'd only start bossing me about, trying to plan my life for me. I've decided I'm going to stand on my own two feet, make my own decisions.'

'You're like your mother,' said Julian. 'On

the strength of one long relationship you base your opinions of us all.' They reached the door. The clock on the wall showed nine o'clock.

'It's still early,' she protested. 'I don't go to bed at nine!'

'Tonight you do. And if you disagree I'll come and put you to bed myself.'

Pippa couldn't stop the shiver that ran through her. Her knees felt weak and she hung on to the door-handle of the car. He was right. She was tired and upset. She'd feel quite different in the morning. He unlocked the car and she climbed inside. Perhaps it was the mead—she was feeling really sleepy and lethargic. She snuggled into her seat and closed her eyes. The steady hum of the car was soothing and relaxing. Within seconds she was back in her flat, and Neil was still there, and he was terribly angry. He held a huge pair of scissors, and he was trying to stab her with them! She cowered in a corner of the kitchen. It wasn't scissors, it was a bread knife—no, it was something on a silver chain, a ring with emerald and diamonds, he was swinging it in front of her eyes, she felt giddy, she was falling, now flying like a butterfly, the butterfly had vivid blue eyes, and it was Neil with a brooch, he jabbed at her, there was blood coming from her hand, lots of blood . . .

She woke with a start, crying out. Still in the dream, she held out her hand and could

142

almost see the blood.

'No—no—no—' Consciousness came suddenly. She sat up in her seat. The car had stopped. Julian sat watching her, a strange expression in his eyes. It seemed such a natural thing to do, to move towards him, into his waiting arms. Her heart was like a sledgehammer, and she could hear his, too, fast but strong.

'I had a dream,' she whispered. He didn't reply but lowered his face to hers. She parted her lips to meet his, and now she was really having a dream. His hands moved over her, caressing and stroking, his lips searched and probed. Pippa felt she was going to burst as she responded. But of course it was a dream. After a few minutes he lifted his mouth from hers, but his arms still held her close.

'It's all a dream,' she whispered.

'No, it's not a dream. It's real.' His blue eyes seemed to shine in the twilight.

'You just feel sorry for me.'

'Why should I feel sorry for you?'

'Because my engagement is over.' He was nuzzling her neck, and kissing it softly, like a butterfly touch. 'Then I should feel sorry for Neil, losing you.'

'You're just saying that.'

His fingers caressed her hair and her ears, and she felt she was in heaven. She had never felt like this with Neil, he had never stirred her senses until she felt she had an erupting

143

volcano inside her. She stroked his neck, and he kissed her fingertips. Their lips touched briefly. Did this ever have to end?

'I think I shall really come and put you to bed,' Julian whispered. 'Is there room for me?'

'There's always room for you.' What had got into her? Her mother had warned her against men like Julian Reed.

But this was delicious, it was ecstasy. Surely her mother couldn't deny her a love like this? She stroked his face, feeling the beginnings of stubble, and he grabbed her hand again, kissing it all over.

'Oh, Pippa!' Their lips met again, in a rush of passion, but eventually, their passion spent, they lay together, sighing blissfully.

'What's happened to my good night's sleep?' Pippa reminded him. 'It was doctor's orders, if I recall.'

'As long as you don't go taking other doctors' orders,' he replied, in the velvet voice she loved so much. With an exaggerated sigh, he opened the car door.

'I'll wait here while you check your flat,' he said. Reluctant to move from his side, Pippa looked up at the windows.

'It's all right. There's someone there. I saw a movement.'

'Neil's waiting for you,' said Julian, taking her hand and kissing it.

'No, it's probably Lucy. She had a split shift.'

'I'm going to have to let you go, then.' They clung to each other, their bodies almost moulded together in the dim twilight.

'Goodnight, Pippa. Think of me.'

'As if I could ever forget you.'

He crossed to his car and got inside. Was that it? thought Pippa. No arrangements to meet again? She'd see him on duty, of course. Yes, there'd be plenty of opportunity to speak.

Her heart singing she ran up the stairs with renewed vigour. The door to her flat was ajar. The place seemed deserted. Where was Lucy?

A strange noise sent her hurrying down to Lucy's door.

'Are you there?' No reply, then the strange moaning noise again. 'Lucy?' She pushed open the door and went inside. The light was off, and the first thing she saw in the dimness was an empty pill bottle on the carpet, then Lucy under the covers, sobbing as though her heart would break.

CHAPTER NINE

'Lucy!' Pippa ran forward and pulled at the counterpane.

'Leave me alone!'

'No, Lucy—what have you done?' She picked up the little bottle and read the label. Sleeping tablets. A hollow settled in her stomach. What had Lucy done? She needed help! She ran to Lucy's window which overlooked the forecourt. Julian's cream car was just nosing around the corner, soon out of sight. 'Damn!' She turned to Lucy, who had uncovered her head and was staring belligerently at her.

'Why are you back so soon? You're not usually back as early as this.' Pippa didn't miss the implications of that remark. Lucy had apparently wanted her to stay out late. Why? So she could do something secret before she came back? Something like . . . She held up the empty bottle.

'How many have you taken, Lucy? You realise you'll have to go to Casualty and have your stomach washed out?'

'Don't be daft. I suggest you put the light on.'

Mystified, Pippa did so. Only then did she see the small white tablets scattered over the carpet. She bent to pick them up.

'This doesn't tell me how many you've taken, Lucy. The bottle could have been full.'

She had found about a dozen and tipped them back into the bottle.

'I haven't taken any . . . I dropped them, and I felt so silly scrabbling after them I decided he just wasn't worth it. No man is.'

A man? thought Pippa.

'So you had planned on taking the lot?'

'The lot. I planned on having a good long

sleep.'

'You'd have had that all right. Where did you get them from?'

'My doctor gave me them. I haven't been sleeping. Oh, leave me alone, Pippa, you're a pain in the neck.'

Looking properly at her for the first time, Pippa saw the pink swollen eyelids, the puffy face and blotchy skin. Lucy had been crying for ages. Pippa's heart went out to her.

'Can't you tell me about it, Lucy? Get it off your chest? I didn't know you were so upset you weren't sleeping. You always seem so cheerful. Well, until lately.'

'I've put on a good face, haven't I?' said Lucy, sitting up and pulling the counterpane up to her neck. Pippa caught a glimpse of her white uniform dress. She hadn't even bothered to change into her night clothes.

'I couldn't tell you about the sleeping tablets. You'd have asked awkward questions. That day, when Neil arrived—' she swallowed '—and you looked for a plaster, I was sure you'd seen them. They were in that box. But you said nothing. Did you think they were aspirins?'

'I didn't see them, Lucy. I wasn't prying.' Just a letter, Lucy. A letter from Neil. But it didn't matter any more.

'It quite scared me for a moment,' said Lucy.

Pippa changed the subject. 'Is it—someone

147

in London?' she asked boldly.

'Who told you? No one here knows. That is—only—' Her lips quivered, and she looked like she was going to burst into tears again.

'No one told me. I put two and two together. Every time you came back from London you seemed low-spirited. I wondered if it were someone you knew when you were working there.'

'There was someone in London. He was the orthopaedic registrar.' She spoke in a low voice. 'I was mad about him.'

'Didn't he—like you?'

'He said he loved me. But he was married. His wife refused to have children, some irrational fear that she'd die.'

'Not an ideal situation,' Pippa agreed, thankful that she'd never fallen in love with a married man. Although she had thought Julian was married in the beginning, but that was before she'd fallen in love with him. Her mouth dropped slightly as the thought registered. Was she really in love with Julian Reed? He certainly did things to her that no other man had ever done.

'He kept telling me she wouldn't divorce him because it was against her religious principles. She was Roman Catholic, you see. He wasn't.'

'Are you sure he really loved you?' As Julian loves me, thought Pippa ecstatically. Julian loves me! She felt like shouting it from the

148

roof-tops. But people would think she'd gone mad. Like Gwen Jordan. Perhaps it was catching, madness.

'I believed he did.' Lucy spoke in a flat unemotional voice. 'But as the months went by I began to realise there was no future in it for me. I'd had enough of the cloak-and-dagger stuff. I wanted someone who could really love me openly. So I left, and came here.'

'But that was eighteen months ago,' said Pippa. 'Aren't you over him yet? Is he still bothering you?'

'I haven't seen him since last September,' said Lucy, hugging her knees. Her blonde hair hung in damp tendrils round her shoulders. Her pillow had a large damp patch in the middle. Pippa couldn't understand how her friend could still be hankering after an old love after so many months' separation.

'I went up to London to see my friends,' said Lucy. 'And we went to a restaurant. And he was there. With a very pregnant lady.'

'So she'd changed her mind? Oh, I'm glad it turned out right for them. But Lucy, you mustn't hanker—'

'It wasn't his wife,' said Lucy. 'Not his first wife, anyway. She'd divorced him just after I left, and he'd married one of the nurses. A girl I knew.'

'Oh, Lucy, that's terrible! You must have been awfully upset.'

'I was. Not with him. I realised then I'd been

eating my heart out for a liar and a cheat. She was welcome to him. No, I hated her for having an affair with him behind my back. She'd always professed dislike for him. So they're a good pair together. An ideal match, you might say.'

Pippa was becoming a little confused. If Lucy wasn't breaking her heart for this orthopaedic Romeo, who was it? She stood up.

'I'll go and make us some cocoa. It will help us to sleep.'

'There's more to tell,' said Lucy. 'And you won't like it.'

'Oh, dear.' Pippa attempted to puzzle out that remark as she waited for the kettle to boil. How could Lucy's problem affect her?

Smiling cheerfully, she took in two mugs of drinking chocolate, and some custard creams she'd found in a box.

'The biccies are a bit soft but they're all right,' she said, setting down the tray. Lucy didn't move to take anything.

'This is going to be hard to say,' she began. 'You know I've always valued your friendship.'

'And I yours,' said Pippa slowly and thoughtfully.

'You know now I'm not moping for Tony, the orthopaedic bod.'

'I gathered that.'

'It was when I discovered the truth about Tony that I realised I was already in love with someone else.'

150

'This sounds more cheering,' said Pippa, biting a biscuit and pulling a face. After all, she could afford to feel cheerful. She was in love, too.

'You won't say that when I tell you. You see, he's in love with someone else, and they're going to get married.'

'Oh, Lucy, I'm so sorry! You do seem to have picked the wrong men.'

'Haven't I just? And you seem to have all the luck, the pick of the men, they all fall at your feet—' She started to cry.

'Please, Lucy, don't feel like that. I'm sure it isn't true. You're young and pretty, I'm sure the right one will come along soon.'

'Platitudes!' snapped Lucy. 'Don't you understand? He has come along. I know there'll be no one else for me. And if I can't have him I may as well be dead!' She wiped her face with the sheet.

'Can't you tell me who he is? Does he work here at the hospital?'

Pippa was desperately trying to remember who was working at the hospital last year, when Lucy fell in love with him. The paediatric housemen were too new, in fact all the housemen were too recent. The registrars—well, it couldn't be Julian, but there was Paul Jackson, yes, he was on the same firm as Julian so he'd go to Ward Six, and yes, he was still single. Funny. She hadn't heard on the grapevine that he'd got engaged.

Lucy was scrabbling under her pillow. She pulled out a pale blue envelope, crumpled and damp in places, and held it out to Pippa.

'You'd better read this.'

With a shock, Pippa recognised the letter she'd found in the shoe box, the airmail letter from Chile. 'I can't read this, Lucy. It's private.'

'Don't you recognise the writing? The ink's run a bit. I've been crying over it. But you should know it.'

'Yes, I do. It's a letter from Neil.' Should she reveal she'd seen it before? No, perhaps it would be better not to.

'I want you to read it, Pippa. I realise I shall probably lose your friendship afterwards, but it's time you knew the truth.'

Reluctantly, Pippa withdrew the single sheet of airmail paper. It was headed, 'Valparaiso, April 12th'.

'Are you sure, Lucy?'

'Positive. Read it.'

The air was thick with tension as Pippa started to read, and Lucy watched her intently.

'Dear Lucy,' Pippa read. 'I was very surprised to receive your letter, particularly after our conversation in the Green Man.'

Pippa caught her breath. The Green Man was where he'd always taken her. She'd always thought it was a special haunt of theirs. She carried on reading, bemused.

'I am sorry you're feeling so bad about it,

152

but I thought you had understood my reasons for what I did. You know I am very fond of you, but you did accept it cannot go any further. I wasn't aware your feeling for me was so deep. I'm sorry—I can't help that. You know I cannot allow our friendship to develop into anything more.

'Please, Lucy, find someone else, you're young and pretty. There must be lots of eligible young doctors at Kingslake. As you say, yes, my feeling for you could quite easily turn into love, but I cannot take that chance. I love Pippa dearly, and I know she feels the same as I do.'

Pippa swallowed, and laid down the letter.

'Have you read it?'

'Not all of it. Lucy—I can't—'

'Please, Pippa.'

Just a few sentences were left. Pippa was finding it painful.

'Please don't write to me again. I shan't reply. It is too embarrassing. If things had been different—but I have to consider Pippa. I expect we shall marry in the near future. So it has to be goodbye, Lucy. I expect I shall see you when I come home, but I shall be grateful if you don't refer to this letter at all. I hate to hurt you, Lucy, but it has hurt me to have to write this. Regards, Neil.'

Slowly, with a feeling of relief, Pippa folded the letter and replaced it in the envelope.

'So it's Neil,' she said flatly. 'All the time

you've been in love with Neil.'

'You can't imagine what it's been like, trying to hide it.' Lucy sat up and hugged her knees. Her eyes were dark with misery.

'It must have been torment to hear me talking about him,' said Pippa. Lucy nodded.

'But when you asked me to go to the airport—'

'I didn't ask you, if you remember rightly. You offered.'

'Did I? I must have been desperate. I never wanted you to know.'

'I'm glad you've told me. It must have been a difficult thing to decide.'

'I suppose you hate me now. But don't worry, I shall get out of your life. Nurse Charles is leaving. I shall take over her flat—'

'Lucy—no—you mustn't. I have to tell you something.' Lucy didn't appear to be listening.

'All the while I was on duty tonight I was imagining you with Neil, eating together, talking together, touching each other—oh, Pippa, what am I going to do?'

'Lucy, Lucy, you don't have to do anything! Listen to me! I'm not going to marry Neil.'

'I don't think I could bear to come to your party, Pippa—What did you say?'

'I said, I'm not going to marry Neil.'

'Is this some sort of joke? It's in very poor taste.'

'That's what Neil said when I told him. Lucy, since he came back I gradually realised things weren't quite the same between us. I'm still very fond of him, and I know I've hurt him deeply, but it was better now than after we were married. I'm not in love with him, Lucy. I don't think I ever have been.'

'But he loves you,' cried Lucy. 'He's told me so many times.'

'Yes, I know,' said Pippa sadly. 'That's why it hurts me as much as him. I hated doing it, Lucy, but I couldn't live a lie.'

'Had you just told him when you came in?' asked Lucy. 'Because you didn't look very unhappy, then.'

'No, Lucy, I told him as soon as I saw him tonight. He was upset, and so was I, and I just couldn't face him any longer. So I—just left him.'

'I suppose you've been walking the streets, hating yourself,' said Lucy sympathetically.

'No. I'll be honest. I—met someone. And he—took me somewhere to cheer me up.'

'He?'

'Well, it's no secret. It was Julian Reed.'

'Julian! I didn't know—'

'There's nothing in it, Lucy. He just—felt sorry for me.'

Pippa didn't understand, herself, why she was denying her love for him, and his for her. But it was too soon to show it to the world. She wanted to keep it secret a little longer, hug it to herself when she was alone.

'So he wanted to cheer you up,' said Lucy

slowly.

'He could see I was upset.'

'And who is going to cheer up Neil? Didn't you stop to consider how he might be feeling?'

'Lucy, Neil was the reason I was upset. But I'm the last person to try to cheer him up.' She looked speculatively at Lucy as a thought occurred to her. 'You could cheer him up, Lucy. He likes you. You love him. He said in the letter he'd find it easy to fall in love with you. Lucy—why don't you ring him? He'll be home by now.'

Lucy shrank back. 'I couldn't, Pippa. He'd feel embarrassed, my knowing you've ended it all. He won't want to see anyone.'

'Perhaps not at first. But knowing how you care, Lucy, he'll need someone to turn to. Please, Lucy, it will make me feel so much better. Just tell him you know what's happened. You needn't mention my name. He's going to need someone to talk to, someone who'll sympathise. Go and ring him, Lucy. Ring him now.'

'All right,' said Lucy, and her eyes were shining, but not with tears.

CHAPTER TEN

The woman in the Admission-Room on the Delivery Suite came awkwardly out of the shower, clutching her cotton dressing gown to her. She grimaced and panted as another contraction began.

Pippa turned from the trolley where she'd been writing her findings.

'You're doing fine, Mrs Field,' she encouraged her. 'Are these your things? Come along, take my arm, we'll get you into your room.'

Mrs Field relaxed as the pain diminished. 'I'm fine, Nurse. You don't have to worry about me. This is my fourth. That's why I came in early. A couple of hours and I expect I'll be ready.'

'So you've got three already,' smiled Pippa, leading her out of the room and into the corridor. It was just small talk. She'd read it in the notes. The youngest was two, the eldest six.

'I've got two boys and a girl. The girl's the eldest. I'm hoping this one's a girl. This is the last.'

'I've heard that before!' laughed Pippa. 'Here we are.'

'I mean it,' said Mrs Field. 'I only intended to have two!'

Pippa saw her into bed, and handed the notes to the pupil who was going to look after her. Then she went back to the Admission-Room to clear up the mess.

This was the first time she'd worked in Admission. She suspected Sister had put her here to get over yesterday's traumatic events.

The bruise on her face was already a lovely purple, but make-up, which she didn't usually wear on duty, had partly disguised it.

Duty on Admission varied. Some days it was really quiet, with only a couple of patients arriving all day. Other days it was hectic, with a dozen or more, and some arriving just in the nick of time. Today, Mrs Field had been the second to arrive. The first lady had arrived as Pippa went on duty. She'd been in a bit of a hurry, and hadn't had time for a shower. At coffee, Jane Marshall had told her she'd delivered at half-past eight.

It was eleven o'clock now, and all was quiet. The room was tidy, all the trolleys prepared for action. She went to the little window and gazed out. Not much of a view; just the side of the hospital and the car park. Some five hundred yards away, the main hospital stood grey and many-windowed in the sunlight. She was glad it was a nice day; she had a half-day and was visiting her mother. Her heart thudded at the thought. Telling Neil it was all off was bad enough, but telling her mother would be worse. If only she had some moral support.

As her gaze travelled back across the car park she caught sight of a familiar cream Rover, and she felt a fluttering inside, and a tingling in her veins. She had gone to bed wondering if she'd really been dreaming. Had she gone to a wine bar with Julian? Had he kissed her as if he meant it? It all seemed vague and woolly now, except for the pressure of his lips. Wishful thinking? She wouldn't know until she saw him again. One look at his face would tell her if it really had happened.

She was jerked out of her reverie by running footsteps, and the door of the Admission-Room was thrust open with a bang. A porter rushed a wheelchair inside, containing a very young, dark-haired girl clutching her huge stomach and making a keening noise.

'Just made it,' puffed the porter. 'Here you are.'

'Got her notes?' urged Pippa, helping the girl into another chair next to the examination table.

'Sorry, she's an emergency, not from round here, not registered at Kingslake.'

'Oh, well, it's not important.' It was, but the girl was looking anxious and tearful, as if she expected to be turned away, not having any records.

'OK, Nurse,' said the porter, and, whistling, he wheeled the chair back to the ambulance bay. Pippa could see the girl was very near to the second stage, if not already there. There was no time to waste.

'We'd better get you out of your things,' she suggested gently. 'Then I can have a look at you. What's your name?'

'Lynsey Peters,' gasped the girl, bending forward and groaning. 'Oh, God, nobody told

159

me it was like this.'

Pippa scribbled her name on a chart, and with difficulty managed to get Lynsey out of her own clothes and into a hospital smock.

'I'm not due yet,' Lynsey explained when the pain had diminished. 'I live in London. I've been staying with my cousin. Then, during the night, the pains started. I was sure it was a false alarm. But—' she bit her lip '—half an hour ago the waters broke. I was soaked.' She tried to laugh. 'Good job it was in the kitchen. Margaret said it looked like the real thing and she got the ambulance. And—oh—I don't know whether I'm sup-posed to, but I've been getting this awful urge to push—oh—'

She struggled on to the table, and Pippa, suspecting the worst, had her fears confirmed. Telling the girl to pant, she tore open a delivery pack on the trolley and pulled on a pair of sterile gloves. There wasn't even time to scrub, because already the baby's head was crowning. Controlling it with her hand, and exhorting Lynsey to pant again, she gently eased it out.

'Nearly over,' she told Lynsey. 'Rest for a moment. The next contraction will push the baby out.' Checking the cord wasn't round its neck, she was surprised at the small size of the baby's head. The girl had said she wasn't due, but she hadn't said how many weeks pre-mature she was. Strange, because she hadn't even looked premature—in fact, very much

160

overdue!

'When are you due?' she asked, watching for restitution of the head, meaning the baby was in the correct position for the body to be born. It was starting to turn.

'In a month. I think—'

'You don't need to push too hard,' advised Pippa, and smoothly and competently she lifted the baby up and out.

'It's a girl,' she said, laying it on a towel. The tiny baby squirmed and opened its mouth, and let out a cry.

'Thank God for that!' cried Lynsey. 'Thank God it's all over.'

Pippa was feeling quite proud of herself, the way she'd delivered the baby without supervision. Then she bit her lip. Would Sister be cross that she hadn't sent for her? But she hadn't had time even to ring the bell for assistance. And she hadn't been able to give the syntometrine, either. She'd give it as soon as she'd cut the cord.

'Is she a big baby?' asked Lynsey. 'Everyone thought I was due last month! Margaret said it was a big baby.'

'She's actually rather small,' said Pippa, wrapping the baby and passing it to Lynsey, who cooed over it and marvelled at its tiny fingernails.

'A lot of water, I expect,' murmured Pippa, drawing up the injection. The door opened then, and Sister came in. She took in the

161

situation at a glance.

'All over?' she asked.

'Except for the third stage,' said Pippa, and swabbed Lynsey's thigh. Lynsey screamed.

'It's all right,' soothed Pippa. 'It's just to help the third stage.'

'No—it's not that—something's happened —down below—oh, I've got an awful pain—'

Just the afterbirth, Pippa was about to say, when she noticed the spreading pool of water between the girl's thighs. Water? It didn't look like urine. Where had it come from?

Sister laid her hand on Lynsey's abdomen, which was still quite round and hard. Her finger on the emergency bell, she said tautly, 'Twins. There's another one. Good job you didn't give the syntometrine. You'd better check its position. It might be breech. I've sent for Dr Reed.'

Aghast, Pippa checked, and sure enough, the head of another baby was visible. She put down the syringe with relief. The injection would have caused the uterus to contract before the baby had been delivered. It could have caused a serious lack of oxygen.

'It's vertex,' she told Sister.

'I thought it was all over,' gasped Lynsey, her face red with exertion. Sister took the baby and placed it in the crib. Couldn't have Lynsey dropping it while she pushed!

'I should have suspected something,' said Pippa. 'Lynsey looked so big, yet the baby was

162

so small.' Sister nodded.

The door opened again, and in strode Julian Reed.

'An extra delivery-room?' he asked jokingly, and his blue eyes rested on Pippa. They seemed to have a message in them, that last night hadn't been a dream.

'Twins, is it?' He peered at the first one.

'We thought the second one might be a breech,' said Sister. 'That's why I rang. But it's vertex, so we shouldn't have any problems.'

He came and stood next to Pippa, and she expected her fingers to become all thumbs. But, to her surprise, she felt quite confident, quite calm. And hadn't she already delivered the first baby without help?

The head was crowning. Lynsey was pushing beautifully, and within a short time another baby girl lay under Pippa's hands, its face contorted and red, making sure everyone knew it had arrived.

At the time Pippa was acutely aware of Julian's gaze on her, but her hands were steady and capable, and she hadn't knocked anything over! She wrapped the baby in a blanket and handed it to Lynsey, who stared at it in amazement.

'I can't believe it!' she gasped. 'No one said I was having two!'

'They're not always diagnosed,' said Sister. 'Not if one is behind the other.' She'd given the syntometrine, Pippa was calmly and carefully delivering the large placenta, much larger than the usual because it had supplied nourishment to two babies.

'Are they identical?' asked Lynsey. 'Oh, golly, what am I going to call them? I was sure it was going to be a boy, not two girls.' She smiled at Pippa. 'What's your name, Nurse?'

Pippa blushed. 'Philippa, but I'm Pippa for short.' She caught Julian's amused gaze and looked away.

'Then one shall be Philippa, Pippa for short.' She glanced at Sister. 'What is—'

'Now you can't call it Doris, not in this day and age,' she said gruffly, with embarrassment.

Pippa caught Julian's eye and grinned cheekily. Boldly, she said, 'But the doctor's name is Julian. Don't you think Julia would be a nice name for the other?'

'It's lovely!' enthused Lynsey. 'I'm sure Gary will be pleased. He likes aristocratic names.'

'Your husband?' asked Sister.

'My boyfriend, but we're getting married next year.'

'That's very nice,' said Julian politely. Lynsey had been tidied up and washed—no suturing had been necessary—and Pippa went to check the babies. They were both perfect, with wisps of dark hair. Lynsey asked again if they were identical. Julian had examined the placenta, and he came across, wiping his hands.

'Yes, they are identical. One chorion,' he

explained to Pippa. Pippa looked across at Lynsey, so tired and happy. She felt a twinge of envy. Sister had gone to arrange Lynsey's admission to one of the wards. Not being a patient of Kingslake, there officially wasn't a bed for her, but a few beds were usually kept for emergencies. She was to go up to Ward Six.

'I know there are a couple of empty beds,' Julian had told Sister. 'And no one expected for a week or two.'

As Pippa cleared away the trolley and prepared it for the next patient, and Lynsey dozed happily, Julian came across to Pippa and touched her arm. A thrill ran through her.

'When are you off duty?' he asked in a low voice, and her knees trembled. She felt breathless.

'I've got a half-day, but I'm visiting my—'

'Dr Reed! Dr Reed!' The door burst open. 'Dr Reed, Mrs Gale has started to haemorrhage!'

Without another glance at Pippa, he hurried from the room. Pippa stood at the trolley, feeling empty inside. What had he been about to say? Offering to take her out? Her chest felt like bursting. She went over to Lynsey, who was admiring her babies with a maternal smile.

'I'll get you a cup of tea,' said Pippa.

'Yes, please. Two sugars,' said Lynsey. 'He's nice, isn't he? The doctor called Julian. I saw the way he was watching you.'

'He can be very critical,' said Pippa,

deliberately misunderstanding.

'It wasn't that sort of look,' said Lynsey, with a sidelong glance.

'I'll get your tea.'

She hurried along to the kitchen where the kettle was always kept boiling. There seemed to be a lot of commotion in Room Three, and the door was ajar. As she emerged from the kitchen with a hot cup of tea, Julian hurried from Room Three, calling back, 'Get her into theatre straight away. No waiting! I'll get the anaesthetist.'

He swept past Pippa without a glance, and she watched his retreating back, loving every inch of him. She sighed. She knew his work came first. It did with all good doctors. She took the tea into the Admission-Room, her disappointment greater than her sense of achievement at delivering her first twins entirely without help.

*   *   *

At lunch, Pippa met Lucy. The latter had had a long conversation with Neil on the phone the night before, and she had returned with stars in her eyes. She wouldn't talk about it, and Pippa had understood. Wasn't it the same with her and Julian? Lucy looked positively blooming as she ate chicken salad and ice cream.

'I've got a day off tomorrow,' she told Pippa.

166

'We—I'm going to Winchester for the day.'

'That will be nice,' said Pippa, chewing fruit salad.

'I've never been to Winchester. Fancy, all the time I've been here, and I've never been to Winchester.'

'I hope you both enjoy it,' said Pippa casually.

'Oh, we will—' She realised what Pippa had said and looked away. She seemed to be afraid to mention Neil in Pippa's presence.

'Do you want coffee?' asked Lucy, getting up.

'Haven't got time. Got a half-day.'

'Going out with—you-know-who?' Why did she seem so wary of Pippa?

'I'm going to Steep. Alone.'

'I hope you both enjoy it,' laughed Lucy.

'I'm going alone,' Pippa insisted. 'Besides, there's nothing in it.' It was too private, too precious, to tell everyone yet.

'See you tonight,' she said, and left the dining-room. There had been no sign of Julian. Performing a Caesarean, no doubt, on Mrs Gale, admitted for placenta praevia.

She dressed in her brown cotton trousers and cream silk shirt, one with short sleeves because of the weather. Her red curls, newly washed, shone like burnished copper around her shoulders. Planning how she would give her mother the news about Neil and herself, she unlocked her car and set off.

Going through the streets of Basingstoke, she was quite pleased with the way her car had been running just lately. Perhaps she wouldn't have to buy a new one. She drew her breath in sharply as it occurred to her that she could have the red Astra after all. She wasn't going to Chile. She wasn't going anywhere. She could stay on at Kingslake until she and Julian—no, she shouldn't plan so far ahead. Things were bound to go wrong. But it was exciting. She could get the new car, get a loan from the bank. She patted the dashboard of the old blue Escort.

'Sorry, old thing, I know you're doing your best, but I've a feeling this can't last. You're past it, you know. You're a bit like those patients who, although you know they're dying, seem to perk up just before the end, and the relatives start thinking optimistic thoughts.'

Don't be morbid, she told herself. You've got no reason to feel morbid. You're in love.

Humming to herself, she reached the outskirts of the town and headed for open country. Changing gear, she noticed that the ignition light had come on, and stayed on. What did that mean? She tried to remember what she'd learned in the few evening classes she'd attended on car maintenance when she'd first bought the car. She hadn't needed them yet. Was it something to do with the engine? Temperature came to mind. And, sure enough, the temperature gauge had started to rise. Oh, hell, this looked like something serious.

She drew up at the side of the road. There was very little traffic about, most of it going towards Basingstoke. She got out and lifted the bonnet. It crossed her mind that if this had been a human body, she'd have soon found out what was wrong. This seemed to be just lumps of iron and tubes and wires. She poked around inside, getting her fingers oily in the process. The sun was hot on her head. Absently, she rubbed the side of her nose. She couldn't see what was wrong. Should she risk driving it back to Basingstoke, to Webber's Garage? How would she get to see her mother? She'd have to ring and explain. Her mother wouldn't be pleased. She'd put off going to Reading on business in order to see her and Neil. Not Neil now. Not Neil again. Pippa felt vague stirrings of regret.

But daydreaming wouldn't get her car repaired. Out of the corner of her eye she noticed a pale car which had passed her only seconds before, turning round and coming back. She turned to look and did a double-take. It was a cream Rover. It had to be coincidence. He was performing a Caesarean. But the car was slowing down behind her. It stopped. And there was no way she could turn the tall dark-haired blue-eyed man who came towards her, into anyone but Julian Reed. Her heart pounding, she straightened up.

'Trouble?'

'Something's wrong. The ignition light came on. Can't see why.'

'Let me look.'

He was very close. She could see little dark hairs on his arms. And he was wearing stone-coloured trousers and a pale blue shirt.

'You'll get your clothes dirty,' she protested.

'They'll clean. Same as jackets.' A little dig about the coffee incident at Heathrow. She watched as he peered inside, touching things.

'Thought as much,' he finally said, straightening up. 'Your fan belt's gone.'

'Oh, no! And I've got to get to Steep. Can I drive it without one?'

'Only for a short way. You'd get overheated. Look, there's a garage about a hundred yards on. Why don't you take it there? They'll probably do it while you wait.'

'Do you think so? I'll do that, then. Thanks for the help.' She knew her words were stilted. But she couldn't stop thinking about last night, and the way he'd kissed her. And her brain didn't seem to be functioning properly. Every time she looked at him she felt electric shocks running through her.

'Shall I hang around until you get it done?'

Was he just being polite? 'But I'm sure you were going somewhere. I'd hate to keep you from whatever it is.'

'Nothing in particular. Stella wasn't expecting me.'

'You were going to see Stella?' Why couldn't she think of something interesting to say? He'd think her an idiot.

'It doesn't matter. I can't leave you stranded. You don't know who might come along offering so-called help.'

'You said it wouldn't take long.'

'It shouldn't. But I was referring to the garage I usually use. I have no idea what this one is like. It's only a small garage. But they should have fan belts. Look, you follow me in your car. Then, when you're all finished, and I know it's been fixed, I'll go my way, and you can go yours.'

He scrutinised her with his lapis lazuli eyes, and she felt her colour rising.

'Go on. Hop in,' he urged her, and crossed to his own car. Skilfully, he turned it to face the other way and slowly started off. Pippa anxiously followed, her eye on the ignition light and the steadily climbing temperature gauge.

Julian's hundred yards turned out to be more than half a mile, but soon the garage came into view, a small shabby affair with the name 'HARVEY'S GARAGE' in scuffed white hand-painted letters. As she drove the car on to the forecourt, which was small and cluttered with oil cans, she was aware of clanking noises coming from the covered garage at the rear. She got out, and walked around, but no one came to see what she

171

wanted. She glanced back at Julian, waiting in his car. Feeling inadequate, she went inside the garage, and found two men in oily overalls, busily working on an old Jaguar.

'Hello?'

They turned and spotted her. One wiped his hands on a rag, but made no attempt to approach her.

'Want something?'

'My fan belt's gone. Can you do it?'

'I can do anything, miss. Where's your car?'

'Just outside. It's an Escort.'

'An Escort. Well, you just leave it there. I'll see what I can do.' He turned back to the Jaguar. Pippa was annoyed.

'I thought you'd be able to do it now. It shouldn't take long.'

'Now?' His brown eyes raked her figure. 'You mean this minute?'

'Well, I am in rather a hurry—'

'I'm sure you are. And we're in a hurry to get this Jag done.'

'Is he waiting for it?'

'Of course he's waiting for it. Been waiting a week, but it's first come first served. That's only fair.'

'Haven't you got someone else who could do it for me?' asked Pippa desperately.

'He's in Spain. On his holidays.'

'A fan belt doesn't take long—'

'That's if I've got one in stock. I shall have to look first, shan't I?' He appeared to come to a decision. 'Look, I tell you what, come back in two hours. I can't say fairer than that, can I?'

'Two hours!'

'Sorry, can't do it any quicker than that. And that's quicker than some garages I could mention. OK? Two hours?'

'Well—I'm not sure—' The man turned away, shrugging his shoulders. He put the rag in his pocket and went back to the Jaguar. Frustrated, Pippa ran across to the Rover, where Julian relaxed in his seat, listening to music. She tapped on the window and he rolled it down.

'It's going to take two hours,' she wailed. 'If I wait I shan't be able to see my mother. Do you think if I take it to a garage in the town it might be quicker?'

'Difficult to say.' He laid a hand on her arm. 'But I've got a better idea. Leave it here. They'll probably charge less than a big place. And I'll take you to see your mother.'

'I can't let you do that!'

'Are you ashamed of me, Pippa? Don't you want your mother to see me?'

'No—it's not that—' Oh, how could she explain he was just the sort of man her mother had warned her about?

'Then do as I say. Tell the man you'll collect it on your way back. How long do you plan to stay at your mother's?'

'Well, I'd planned on a couple of hours at least.' She paused. 'But it could be a lot less.'

'Right. Run and tell him then.'

Pippa bit her lip. It sounded very much as if he was telling her what to do. Another bossy male. Yet what he said made sense. It was the only way she could get to Steep. She couldn't let her mother down.

She went back to the garage. The men were making an awful din, banging on the Jaguar with mallets.

'I'll leave it,' she shouted, and the brown-eyed one turned and cupped his ear. 'I'm getting a lift, so I'll collect my car later this afternoon. Is that all right?'

'Yeah! Sure!'

He turned back to his hammering, and Pippa ran across the forecourt to the Rover. The door was open and she climbed in gratefully.

'You've got a smut on your nose,' said Julian, as he waited for her to close the door and make herself comfortable.

'Oh! Why didn't you tell me before? No wonder that awful little man was grinning.'

'Only just noticed.' He seemed in no hurry to start, but watched with interest as she dampened a tissue and rubbed it on the offending spot. 'Anyway, I thought it only made you look even more adorable.'

He leaned across and kissed her on the cheek, before starting the car.

Pippa sat like something turned to stone. She couldn't breathe. All night and all

174

morning she'd been sure she had dreamt of his kisses in the car. Then he'd given her such a meaningful look in the Admission-Room, and had come to talk to her afterwards. Yet still she'd doubted. Now he had confirmed it, and she felt so full of joy and love it was in danger of bursting out of her. Hardly daring to speak, in case she said something stupid, she sat and watched the road ahead.

'You haven't fastened your seatbelt.' His left hand gestured towards it, and brushed against her own. Where it touched her skin felt like fire. She adjusted her seatbelt with the silliest notion that now she was fastened in and at his mercy. It made her shiver.

'You're not cold? You haven't brought a jacket.'

'No, I'm lovely and warm. It was just someone walking over my grave.'

'How morbid you are today! Aren't you happy?'

'Blissfully happy.' It was unbelievable how natural it felt, to be sitting next to him. And to know she was secure in his love. The warmth of her feeling spread through her and she gave a sigh of pure happiness.

'Regrets?' he queried, not taking his gaze off the road.

'I don't regret anything.'

'Not giving him up?'

'I wasn't thinking of him.'

'You gave a big sigh.'

'It was a sigh of happiness.' He smiled, and his left hand moved from the wheel and took hers. It felt strong and warm. Impulsively, she lifted it to her lips and kissed it.

'Careful,' he said teasingly. 'People will start thinking you're in love.'

Of course he was joking. He knew she was in love. They travelled a couple of miles without speaking. There seemed to be no need for words.

'Did you say Steep?' Julian finally said.

'Yes. You're going in the right direction!'

'Do you go through Alton?'

'Yes, there's a B road from Alton,' said Pippa. 'It goes through Selbourne and Empshott.'

'I know it. Isn't it the road to Petersfield? I have a friend in Petersfield.'

'Steep isn't far from Petersfield. You take the road from Liss.'

'Liss rhymes with kiss,' said Julian, in a light tone, and glanced at Pippa.

'Liss, kiss. It sounds like Gwen Jordan,' said Pippa quickly, trying to stem the tide of emotion that welled up at his look. It just wasn't fair that he should have such beautiful eyes. They ruined her concentration.

'I was surprised to see you,' said Pippa, when she'd calmed down. 'I was under the impression you were performing a Caesarean.'

'Mrs Gale? Yes, I did. But speed was of the essence in her case. We didn't want the baby to

176

be anoxic. And surely you must have realised by now, I'm not in the habit of hanging about when babies' lives are at risk.'

'Like Amy,' said Pippa softly.

'Like Amy. Poor kid. We had to fight to get compensation for it. We won, but money can't make Amy normal, although it will certainly help when she's older. And it means Stella can get specialised help now, and trained people.'

'Does she go to a special school?'

'Most days. It's too early to say whether it's going to be any use.' His knuckles were white on the wheel. Pippa changed the subject.

'Was Mrs Gale's baby alive?'

'Just about. Very shocked. It went to Special Care, and only time will tell, I'm afraid.'

'Have you saved all the distressed babies you've found?'

'No, damn it, I haven't. You can't save them all. Sometimes the damage is done before you get to them, before you even see the mothers. And some babies it's just impossible to help. We just have to fail sometimes.'

Pippa bit her lip. 'I feel I failed with Gwen Jordan. I should—'

'You did not fail! You saved her baby from harm. You saved it at risk to yourself. Just look at that bruise.'

'I thought I'd hidden it.' She touched her cheek.

'You could only hide that with a yashmak!'

'I wonder what Mother will think when she

177

sees it.'

'Perhaps she'll think Neil did it, and that's why it's all over.' There was a chuckle in his voice.

'I told you—'

'I know. You're still carrying a torch for him.'

'I'm not! But I don't hate him. I could never hate him. I'm still fond of him, and I hate myself for hurting him.'

'His wounds will heal. He'll find someone else.' He glanced at her. His voice was so quiet she could hardly hear the words. 'You won't ever hurt me, will you, Pippa?'

Pippa felt a great lump come into her throat. She could hardly speak. 'Do I mean—that much to you?'

'Didn't you know? Couldn't you tell?'

'Yes—I thought—but then I remembered you don't like redheads. Not since—Stella said you had a thing about them,' she ended lamely. She'd almost mentioned Olivia.

'I do have a thing about them. I can't resist them. As soon as I saw you at Heathrow—'

'But you thought I was' There was a pregnant pause.

'Olivia?' The name dropped like a stone. Pippa held her breath.

'That's what you called me,' she said carefully.

'Did I? That was just from the back, if I remember.' He drove on without speaking. His jaw looked tense. Pippa could have cursed herself for bringing Olivia into the conversation. She'd tried so hard not to, and it had just slipped out.

But now they had reached Liss, and were travelling along the narrow road towards Steep.

'Nearly there,' said Pippa, with a false cheerfulness.

'Perhaps it would be better if I dropped you here, and came back for you in a couple of hours,' suggested Julian.

'You'll do no such thing! You can't hang around all afternoon, waiting for me. You can come and meet my mother.' And I don't care what she thinks!

'I'm looking forward to it. Is she like you?'

'Not a bit! I'm supposed to take after my father. But I don't know. I don't remember him. And Mother threw away all his photographs.'

'Is she still bitter?' asked Julian discerningly.

'I think she is.' And I wonder what she'll make of you?

They passed a row of brick cottages. 'This is it. The thatched one,' said Pippa. Julian drew up outside the cottage and turned off the engine.

'Picturesque,' he commented. 'I'm surprised you ever wanted to leave it.'

'It wasn't the cottage I needed to leave,' said Pippa awkwardly. 'I love my mother, but it was her I had to get away from. I needed to find myself. Does that sound pretentious?'

'Not really.' He looked at her reflectively. 'Let's go in. I think she's at the door.'

Trembling with anticipation, Pippa went first up the short, flower-lined path. Her mother looked puzzled as she kissed and hugged Pippa.

'I thought at first Neil had hired a different car,' she said with a slight frown. 'But this isn't Neil. Where's Neil, Pippa? You said you were both coming to talk to me. About the wedding, I assumed.'

'I'll tell you all about it inside, Mother. This is Julian. He very kindly offered to bring me when my car broke down. He's a doctor from the hospital.'

Julian stepped forward, holding out his hand. Eleanor appraised him for a moment before doing the same. He held it for a long time, looking into her eyes. Eleanor smiled vaguely, looking troubled.

'From the hospital,' she repeated.

'Yes, I'm quite new at Kingslake. Started this month.'

'You'd better come in.' She seemed to find it difficult to take her eyes from his face.

They went inside and sat down, Julian stretching out his long legs.

'Help me with the tray, please, Pippa,' called her mother from the kitchen. Pippa glanced at Julian. Her mother must have called her for quite another reason. She was fully aware how rude it was to leave a guest alone.

'My mother—' she began.

'That's all right. There are a lot of things here to keep me occupied until you get back.' He reached out for a half-finished picture. Pippa went into the kitchen and found her mother standing by the window looking out.

'I don't know what it is you've got to tell me about Neil,' she said in a disturbed way, and turned to look at her. 'But I just know it's got something to do with this Julian fellow. Oh, Pippa, be careful! He's too attractive, too charming. Pippa, he's so much like your father!'

CHAPTER ELEVEN

Eleanor had spoken in a penetrating whisper. Pippa glanced anxiously at the sitting-room door. It was slightly ajar.

'Mother, he's not a bit like Dad,' she said quietly.

'How do you know? You don't remember him.'

'You've always said I'm like him.'

'I'm not talking about looks. And his eyes weren't green, they were blue. No, I'm talking about his charm; the way he looks at one, that understanding expression in his eyes, as if you're the only one who matters. He'll twist you round his little finger if he wants to.'

He already has, thought Pippa. Aloud, she said, 'Mother, you've seen him for a few seconds, how can you possibly judge? And, anyway, Julian's only here because my car broke down.'

The excuse sounded flimsy, even though it was true.

'So he brought you all the way here, just because he knew your car had broken down. He must think a lot of you to do that.'

Her mother's gaze was discerning, and Pippa flushed. Was she really so transparent?'

'He's just a colleague. Just a friend.'

Her mother snorted and began banging the best china on a tray.

'Mother, you'll break it. Let me help.'

'You'd better go and talk to your friend. It's rude to leave him alone in there.'

'But it was you who asked . . .' Her mother turned her back on her and pulled open the cutlery drawer. It was no use, thought Pippa, she'd somehow put her mother in a bad mood, and she'd just have to hope Julian's charm and fascination would improve matters.

Julian was admiring the top picture of a pile sitting on a sheet of brown wrapping paper, the collection her mother had intended taking to Reading before her change of plans.

'These are beautiful,' he remarked. 'Your

mother's work?'

'A little hobby of hers. It fills the hours.'

Julian turned and looked at her. 'Why do you belittle it? It seems to be a very worthwhile occupation.'

'Sorry. I didn't mean to knock it.'

'Is she cross with you for bringing me instead of Neil? She's very fond of Neil, isn't she?'

How did he always seem to size up situations so quickly? He'd make a good psychiatrist, Pippa thought. He'd be able to read the patients' thoughts! Or was it just hers he could read? Were they on the same wavelength? She'd heard of deeply committed couples who always seemed to know what their partners were thinking. She had never felt like that about Neil. He didn't seem to have understood her at all. He seemed to know Lucy better.

'I don't think she's cross,' said Pippa, defending her mother. 'But she's puzzled because she was expecting Neil, and I haven't told her yet why he hasn't come.'

'I think that's the signal for me to go,' said Julian tactfully. 'Look, you can't tell her about Neil while I'm here. And I've just remembered a birthday card I should have bought. It's Stella's birthday in a couple of days. I'll slip into Petersfield. It's not far. And it will give you and your mother time to discuss everything. I suspect she's going to be very

183

disappointed at your news.'

'You're right. She is very fond of Neil. But stay for a cup of tea. It's here now.'

She opened the door as her mother came in with the tray, holding tea and a plate of hazelnut wafers.

'How did you know, Mrs Garland?' exclaimed Julian, taking the tray and placing it on a small table.

'I'm sorry?' She glanced cautiously at him.

'My favourites. Hazelnut wafers, if I'm not mistaken.'

'My late husband liked them too,' said Eleanor stiffly, as if that was a good enough reason to dislike him. She began to pour.

Julian was sensible enough not to pursue the subject. Instead, he remarked on the artistry of her pictures, and the clever colour scheme of the room. Pippa hid a smile. But Julian's beguiling ways soon brought Eleanor out of her bad mood, and soon she was smiling and asking him about the hospital, and his family. Still susceptible, thought Pippa. Within a short time her mother had learned more about Julian than she had in days.

Julian seemed quite happy to talk. And Pippa was quite happy to listen.

'So you work with Pippa, do you?' asked Eleanor, handing him another hazelnut wafer, which he accepted.

'I do. And she's a very competent midwife, even though she's not qualified yet.' Pippa blushed, and stared at her cup of tea. How could he embarrass her like this?

'Did you know she delivered twins this morning, without any help at all? All on her own? And it was the first time she'd done it?'

He knew he was embarrassing her. There was a definite twinkle in his eye as he glanced at her.

'Did you really, Pippa? All on your own? Oh, I'd have been terrified!'

'It wasn't really difficult,' said Pippa modestly, aware that it sounded boastful. 'I mean, they both came head first, there weren't any problems.' She turned to Julian. 'And don't forget I very nearly gave the syntometrine before the second twin appeared.'

'True. But that could have happened to anyone.' He was looking at her with an intimate expression in his eyes, and Pippa was suddenly aware that her mother was watching them with a slight frown. Surely she must suspect something! If only he wouldn't look at her like that, those meaningful glances.

She was relieved when Julian got up and made his excuses about the birthday card. Pippa saw him to the door, and he squeezed her hand.

'I shan't dawdle,' he whispered. 'I shan't leave you together for too long. Hope she doesn't pulverise you. Stand up to her. It's your life.'

Pippa smiled tremulously, and he kissed her

softly on the lips before going down the path. Her chest bursting with happiness, she watched him go, then returned to her mother who was piling the china on the tray. Eleanor didn't even turn as she said, 'What happened to Neil? Why didn't he come?'

Pippa swallowed. She recalled Julian's words.

'I've broken off the engagement, Mother.'

Her mother slowly placed a cup on a saucer with fastidious accuracy, then sat down. 'I guessed something had happened. I guessed the other day when you were so quiet.'

'It only happened yesterday,' said Pippa.

'But you must have been thinking about it. It isn't the sort of decision you can make in a minute.'

'Well, I did,' said Pippa. 'I suddenly realised I wasn't in love with him, I've never been in love with him.'

Eleanor stared at her. 'Don't be silly. Of course you were in love with him. I expect you still are. It's just a silly tiff you've had. You'll make it up. And if you don't want to marry him just yet, you don't have to. You can wait until next summer. Perhaps I did push you a little for an early wedding. There's no rush.' She smiled confidently at Pippa.

'Mother, I don't want to marry Neil at all. Not next summer. Not ever. I still like him a lot, but it isn't enough for marriage. Didn't we talk about this before?'

186

'If we did I don't remember.'

'You don't want to remember. Why don't you want me to have what you had with Dad? Surely you haven't forgotten what it was like, heartstopping ecstasy when he kissed you, fire in your veins when he touched you, your knees turning to water when he called your name? Mother, I want that, too.'

'You've got it all wrong. That's infatuation.'

'But isn't that how you felt with Dad? Didn't the earth move when he kissed you? Wasn't it like a volcano—'

'Pippa, it was a long time ago.' But Pippa had noticed the way her cheeks had flushed, and the way she couldn't meet her eyes.

'You didn't think it was infatuation then, did you? You believed it was love, didn't you?'

'Of course I thought it was love. But I see now it wasn't.'

'It was love, Mother! That's why it made you so bitter, because your love was rejected. If it had been infatuation you'd have forgotten quickly and found someone else.'

'Pippa, you speak as if you know—'

'And, Mother, I think you still love him. Even though he's dead.'

There was a long silence. Eleanor surreptitiously wiped her eyes. Pippa picked up the tray and took it into the kitchen. Her mother followed her, looking wan and dejected. Pippa felt guilty at causing her mother pain, but it was time she faced up to

187

the truth, instead of hiding behind a show of bitterness.

Pippa put the china into a bowl of soapy water, and began to wash the cups.

'So it's really all over,' said Eleanor, behind her.

'It's all over. I hated doing it but I couldn't live a lie.'

'I suppose honesty and pain is better than a lifetime of regrets,' said Eleanor softly.

'I'm glad you understand, Mother,' said Pippa, and, turning, saw tears in her mother's eyes. 'Oh, Mother!' They hugged each other tearfully.

'Pippa, you've got soap suds all over my neck,' complained Eleanor, gruffly, and dabbed at it with a tea towel. As Pippa turned back to her task, her mother said quietly, 'Is it Julian?'

Pippa took a deep breath. She wanted to shout it from the roof-tops that she was in love with Julian Reed, but her instinct told her it was still too fragile, too precious, like a new-born baby. It needed nurturing and protection.

So she said slowly, 'I'd rather not talk about it at the moment. Not yet, Mother. Do you understand? I have to be sure.'

Her mother was busy drying a saucer. 'All right, Pippa. I can wait. When you're ready.'

They finished in silence. As Eleanor placed the last cup on a rack, she said in a light voice. 'He's got lovely eyes, hasn't he?' And then the doorbell went, and Pippa hurried to let him in.

* * *

Next morning, when Pippa went on duty, she was stopped by Sister Brayford before she reached the office for report.

'Nurse Garland, I've been asked by the SNO if I can spare someone quite senior for one of the wards. There's this wretched summer flu epidemic, and everywhere's short except here, apparently. I wonder, do you mind? I hate losing you, you did really well yesterday with those twins. But orders are orders.'

'One of the wards?' echoed Pippa, with some trepidation. If she were sent to One, Two or Three, she'd never see Julian, and he wouldn't even know where she was.

'Ward Six,' said Sister.

'How long for?'

'No idea. Until the sick nurses are back, I suppose.'

'I'd better go, then.' She fetched her cloak from the cloakroom. It wasn't so bad. Wards Four, Five and Six were where patients on Julian's firm were sent, so he'd have to come along for ward rounds with the consultants. And he would be called on for problems. She'd see him now and again. But not nearly as often as being on the Delivery Suite.

She had a sudden, irrational idea that the

189

SNO knew of their love for each other, and was testing that love by separating them. But how foolish. If the SNO was aware of all of Pippa's romantic affairs, she'd believe it to be Neil Chappell. Surely it was too soon for the news of the broken engagement to be around the hospital? Knowing the efficiency of the grapevine, it wouldn't be long.

She ran up the stairs to Ward Six, feeling quite energetic. The day staff were assembled in the office, and Pippa quickly took her seat. Staff Midwife Wellings, who had been on duty all night, sat down with the Kardex on her knee and began to read.

Ward Six, like all the other wards, occupied a whole floor, and was divided into two; an antenatal ward, and a larger postnatal ward and nursery. In the centre of these wards was the office and nurses' station.

Each side was subdivided into four-bedded rooms and four single rooms, the latter for cases that needed isolation or privacy.

Staff Midwife Wellings read through the report, and glanced at the new members of staff.

'Three for discharge today,' she said, flipping the pages, and mentioned their names. 'Mrs Patel is a bit upset, but it's probably because she can't talk to the other mothers. The interpreter is coming along this morning to try to sort out some of her problems. Baby Jenkins's eye seems to be responding to the antibiotic, and Baby Yates, the Down's Syndrome baby, is feeding better. Yesterday's admission on the AN side is still being sick. I've a hunch it's psychological. Her husband hasn't visited, but she seems very light-hearted about it. I sense she's hiding something. That's Mrs Munro.

'Mrs Carby's blood-pressure is still raised, so she can't go home yet. I think that's all the problems. We shall have four empty PN beds, and still three AN beds. No doubt they'll soon fill up.'

She laughed and closed the Kardex, turning to Felicity White, the Day Sister.

'Have a nice day!' She picked up her cloak and bag and left the room. Sister White looked around at the assembled nurses.

'Right, babies first. Nurse Turner, Nurse Lord, will you do the baths? And will you show Mrs Kelly again? She can't seem to get the hang of it. She is very young, and, unfortunately, not terribly bright. Still, she adores her baby and that's the important thing. I expect she'll muddle through once she gets home. As long as she doesn't drown the poor little thing!' The nurses tittered.

'Nurse Potter, the AA tests. I think there are two, the Caesareans due home tomorrow. Nurse Poole, supervise the baths, please, then the dressings. Perineal sutures out for Mrs Hale and Mrs Millington, and clips from the Caesarean ladies. I see we've been sent Nurse

Garland.' Pippa flushed. 'Perhaps you'd do the recordings, please, and find out if there are any problems I don't know about. Oh—and do try to get Mrs Warner to move about more. She's a six-day Caesarean, and if she doesn't start walking around she's going to be in trouble. The physiotherapist is doing her best, but she can't be here all day. Right, is everyone happy?'

There were murmurs; possibly of agreement, possibly not. Pippa was relieved she hadn't been given the AA tests to do, on the babies. These tests for metabolic diseases were usually done after the babies had gone home, by the district midwife, but if the mothers had to stay longer, because of Caesareans or infections, the tests had to be done on the ward. And Pippa hated stabbing the babies' heels, particularly if they were cold or the circulation wasn't good, because then the blood wouldn't flow easily, and didn't the babies complain!

Outside the office, the nurses dispersed to do their various tasks. Pippa collected the sphygmomanometer from its usual place at the end of the nurses' station, and wheeled it into Room A, a four-bedded ward.

At the first bed, a girl in a red cotton dressing gown was bending over a cot. She was small and thin with long dark hair. As Pippa entered the room, she turned, and a look of pleased surprise crossed her face.

'Why, hello! Fancy seeing you here!'

Pippa did a double-take. Then she laughed. Of course, the girl with the twins. With all the hassle of the emergency delivery, she'd not had much time to talk to the girl, and in any case, women in labour frequently looked quite different afterwards. Pippa now recalled Julian saying there were empty beds in Six.

'Lynsey Peters! I'd quite forgotten you'd been sent up here,' she said, glancing at the girl's chart. 'You seem to be doing very well on your first day.'

'Oh, I'm fit as a fiddle. I'm never ill,' Lynsey assured her.

'You're going to need all your health and strength with those two,' commented one of the patients, a middle-aged lady. Pippa glanced at her. She seemed much older than the other women. Could she be the mother of the Down's Syndrome baby? Mrs Yates? She'd soon find out.

She quickly did Lynsey's recordings, which were normal.

'Let me have a look at those babies,' she said. 'Now they've got over the shock.' She peeped into the cribs. Both babies had dark hair and tiny rosebud mouths.

'They're quite exquisite,' she commented, and Lynsey beamed.

'This one's Pippa, the older by five minutes. This one's Julia.'

'She thought those names up quickly,'

remarked another patient, a young angular woman with glasses. 'I've had my baby three days and I still can't make up my mind whether to have Emerald or Amber.'

The middle-aged woman grimaced, and hid a smile.

'I didn't have to choose,' said Lynsey, climbing into bed and picking up a magazine. 'I had it done for me. Philippa—Pippa, really—after Nurse here who delivered them—'

'You delivered the twins?' The angular woman seemed surprised. 'I thought doctors did that.'

'She did it as well as any doctor,' said Lynsey staunchly, and Pippa flushed with embarrassment. 'So I've called one baby after her, and the other after the doctor who came just too late.'

'A lady doctor? Which one was that? There's a young sandy-haired one—'

'No, his name's Julian,' said Lynsey. To her amazement Pippa could feel her cheeks growing warm.

'Let's take your blood pressure, Mrs West,' she said quickly. The angular woman sat on the edge of her bed and obediently held out her arm.

'I'm surprised they didn't send for the doctor to deliver the twins,' she said, as Pippa pressed the Velcro edges of the cuff together.

'Not enough time,' said Pippa. 'They arrived

194

as soon as she got inside the Admission-Room.'

'That's a nasty bruise you've got on your face, Nurse,' remarked the middle-aged woman. 'Boyfriend trouble?'

'Patient trouble,' said Pippa shortly. 'Now can I listen to this pulse, please?'

'Oh, sorry.' She went back to her bed and stood for a while looking down at the baby in the crib. A sigh escaped her.

Pippa had observed her actions while checking Mrs West's pulse, and she was pretty sure her guess had been right.

'Well, you're OK, Mrs West,' she announced cheerfully, filling in the details on the chart.

'Going home tomorrow,' said Mrs West. 'I wish I could make up my mind about Emerald or Amber. You know, I've taken a fancy to Julia. Sounds rather posh, doesn't it?'

She collected her towel and toilet bag and disappeared into the bathroom.

'Sounds rather posh, doesn't it?' mimicked the middle-aged lady, as Pippa reached her bed. Her suspicions had been correct. One glance at the tiny baby in the crib revealed the slanting eyes and small mouth of Down's Syndrome. Baby Yates. She smiled cheerfully at Mrs Yates. She remembered what Sister had said. First baby at forty-two, refused amniocentesis in early pregnancy which would have identified the problem.

'Gets on your wick,' Mrs Yates muttered as

195

Pippa glanced at her chart. 'Emerald. Amber. Why can't she have a sensible name like Susan or Jane?'

'Perhaps she likes the exotic names,' said Pippa tactfully, wrapping the cuff around Marjorie Yates' plump upper arm.

'Exotic names! Silly names.' She sniffed, and a single tear rolled down her cheek.

'Are you all right?' asked Pippa with concern.

'Don't worry about me. I'm just a bit low. A bit irritable. Once I've got used to the idea . . .' She tightened her trembling lower lip. Pippa quickly finished the recordings and sat on the edge of the bed. Lynsey had left the ward, and the other patient, Mrs Warner, seemed to be asleep.

'Do you want to talk about it?' she asked gently.

'There's nothing to say, really.' Mrs Yates picked at the counterpane. 'I had so many dreams when I was young. I always imagined the knight in shining armour coming to sweep me off my feet. I suppose I'm a romantic at heart. Well, he was a long time coming, that's all I can say. I don't know why. I'm not that bad-looking, am I, Nurse? I'm not ugly?'

'No, Mrs Yates. You're not the slightest bit ugly. You've got nice eyes and a nice smile.'

'Homely, I suppose. Gerald says I'm homely. But I still wanted all that the pretty girls wanted, a husband, a home, children—'

She hesitated, her lips quivered. Pippa waited. 'I suppose living at home with my mother didn't help. She was cantankerous to say the least. I suppose it put them off, the men I took home. Well, Mother died three years ago, and I met Gerald at the funeral. A friend of a cousin, or something. Better late than never, I thought. His first wife died young, without children. We both wanted children.' Her voice broke. 'I did so want my dream to come true,' she whispered. Pippa laid a hand on her shoulder.

'I was over the moon last Christmas,' Mrs Yates continued. 'I'd just had it confirmed. I was pregnant! Gerald was really chuffed! So we didn't really listen when they told us of the risks. They suggested I had an amni— something—you know, a test of the water, in case the baby was abnormal. I wouldn't hear of it. There weren't any abnormal babies in my family. My sister has got three lovely grown-up daughters. Why shouldn't mine be the same? I wouldn't listen. So it came as more of a shock when they told me.'

'When did they tell you?'

'Well, they didn't, not right at first. They gave him to me to hold, and I didn't notice their glances, I was too excited. Then I looked at him hard, and I wondered about his eyes. They seemed to slant. But lots of babies do, don't they, at first?'

'They do, Mrs Yates.'

'And I looked at his hands. And I called the nurse over, and I said, "Just look at that, nurse. He's only got one crease on his palms. Isn't that unusual?" And the doctor came over to me. And he was so kind, and so gentle, I'll never forget his sympathetic blue eyes . . .'

Pippa's heart gave a jolt. Julian?

'What did he say, Mrs Yates?'

'He said, "It's not really unusual, not in a baby like this." Like this! And then I think I realised. It was a terrible shock, even though he'd not actually told me. They sent in Gerald, and I could tell by his face they'd told him something, but he said I wasn't to worry, he was a lovely baby and quite healthy. He is healthy, isn't he, Nurse?'

She stared at the crib wistfully.

'Yes, Mrs Yates, he seems to be a lovely, healthy baby. Yes, I mean that. You mustn't listen to well-meaning people who tell you it's a tragedy, and he should be in an institution, he'll always be an imbecile. Down's Syndrome children are lovely children; they're happy, placid, musical, and more than that, they're lovable and loving. You'll always have your son, Mrs Yates. He'll never go and leave you. And it's amazing what can be done these days. Some of them, no, a lot of them, learn enough to hold down a simple job.'

'Is that so, Nurse?' Mrs Yates' eyes widened. 'When I was a child, there was a home for them near to where we lived then, and I saw them, drooling and shuffling, with vacant eyes. I don't want Paul to be like that!'

'I'm sure he won't be, Mrs Yates. I expect someone will come and see you before you leave here, and they'll keep in touch, and you'll be able to meet other mothers like yourself. You won't believe what they achieve these days. I know of a Down's Syndrome girl who passed her driving test.'

Mrs Yates' eyes were shining. 'Is that true? Oh, I'm so glad you stopped to talk to me. I was imagining the worst. I was feeling so miserable.'

Pippa touched the baby in his crib, and a tiny hand grasped her finger.

'See that, Mrs Yates? He's doing just the same as a normal baby.' Mrs Yates gave a tremulous smile, and by the time Pippa had reached Mrs Warner's bed, she was standing by the crib, her finger in her son's tiny fist, and a smile on her face.

But Pippa's attention was on Mrs Warner, dozing in the last bed. She turned as Pippa approached, and a fleeting grimace crossed her face.

'All right, Mrs Warner? I've just come to do recordings.'

'Oh, yes, Nurse.' She moved carefully and slowly into a sitting position and held out her arm. Pippa read the chart. Six-day Caesarean. And someone had written in large red letters—'ENCOURAGE MOVEMENT'!

'Has the physiotherapist been yet?' she asked, knowing full well it was too early in the day.

'Not yet, Nurse.' Iris Warner's voice was weak and whiney.

'Have you been walking about this morning?'

Blood-pressure was fine. Pulse a little rapid. The slight rise in temperature a couple of days ago had subsided.

'I've been to the bathroom, Nurse. But it's very painful still. Takes me ages just to get out of bed. She was a breech, you see, and I've got ever such a big incision.'

'Yes, I know all that, Mrs Warner, but you must get up and walk about. It's important for your circulation. Very important after a Caesarean.'

'Oh, my circulation's fine, Nurse. I will start walking about when I feel a bit better.'

'So, no aches or pains then? Legs all right?'

'Oh yes—well, I had a bit of cramp yesterday, but it went away.' Pippa put down the chart and made to leave the room. Something caused her to pause and look back at Mrs Warner.

'I'd better check,' she said.

'Check what?'

'Your legs. Where you had the cramp.'

'But it's gone now. Left a bit of an ache, but it's not too bad.'

'I really have to check.'

'Oh, all right. Can't understand it. Nobody seems bothered about all the stitches and clips I've got. More interested in my legs. Seems daft to me.'

She pulled back the sheets to reveal pale, bony legs and knobbly feet. Pippa gently palpated the calf of the nearest leg. Iris Warner watched her dispassionately.

'It wasn't that leg,' she said flatly, when Pippa had finished.

Holding back her annoyance, Pippa examined the other leg. And as she gently stroked the calf Mrs Warner let out a cry.

'That's where it was. It only hurts when you touch it.' With the words deep vein thrombosis running through her head, Pippa calmly replaced the sheets.

'I'll get the doctor to look at it.'

'Is it bad?'

'You've had it since yesterday?' asked Pippa. 'Didn't anyone ask you about it? Didn't they ask you if your legs were all right?'

Iris Warner looked craftily at Pippa.

'I'm not sure they did. They don't always ask—'

'Yes, they do,' said Marjorie Yates firmly. 'Like you, Nurse, they all ask about our legs.'

'I don't remember,' said Mrs Warner in a weak voice, and pulled herself up the bed. Suddenly, she let out a cry and clutched at her chest. Pippa's heart leapt.

'What's wrong?'

201

'A pain—in my chest—I can't breathe—' Her skin had rapidly changed to a pale greyish hue, and her lips were mauve.

Pulling the curtains round the bed, Pippa pressed the emergency bell three times. Then she turned on the oxygen, which was conveniently fixed to the wall behind the bed.

Iris Warner was quiet now, collapsed against the pillows. Soon the oxygen mask was over her face, and she gulped at it greedily. The ward doors opened with a bang and Sister White appeared between the curtains. One glance told her what had happened. 'Pulmonary embolism?' Pippa nodded.

'I'll get Dr Reed.' She hurried away, and Pippa continued her task of keeping the woman as comfortable as possible. Her pulse had risen, and she was having great difficulty in breathing. There was fear in her pale eyes as she opened them and looked at Pippa. She attempted to say something, but Pippa patted her arm and said, 'Don't try to talk. Save your energy. You're doing fine.' Her earlier irritation with the woman had disappeared. Now she needed her help. She was glad the woman couldn't talk. If she'd asked her what was wrong she'd have been loath to tell her the truth. Knowing she had a blood clot in the lung wouldn't be conducive to tranquillity!

Rapid footsteps came from the corridor and into the room. The curtains were thrust aside and Julian strode across to the bed. His fingers on Mrs Warner's pulse, he turned to Pippa.

'When did this happen?'

'Oh—two or three minutes ago. I'd been looking at her legs because she said—'

But Julian wasn't listening. He turned to Sister White. 'Morphine, please, Sister, and heparin.'

Sister White had come well prepared. Behind her on the trolley lay a drip set and a small covered tray. Julian quickly drew up the required drugs.

'Morphine, fifteen milligrams,' he said. 'Hold her arm, Pi—Nurse Garland.'

Pippa had noticed his slip of the tongue. Anxiously, she glanced at Sister White, but she was writing on the chart. Within minutes, the drip was up, and the drugs given.

'I've given twenty thousand units of heparin,' said Julian. 'We'll have to see how she goes. We'll give the heparin four-hourly for the next forty-eight hours. Keep her legs elevated, Sister, and make sure she moves them. That's what's caused this trouble.'

The morphine had started to take effect, and Mrs Warner drowsed happily, hardly aware of the seriousness of the situation.

'She ought to be specialled,' said Julian, once he was satisfied he could do no more, and he glanced at Pippa. She felt the familiar tingling in her veins, and a longing to touch him.

'I'll get Nurse Turner to do it,' said Sister as

she left the ward with him. Pippa stayed by the bedside, her eyes on the drip and Mrs Warner's breathing, which had eased slightly. The woman slept. Nurse Turner slipped between the curtains.

'I've come to take over,' she said. 'Sister wants to see you.'

Pippa found Sister with Julian in the office. Julian was voicing his concern over Mrs Warner's reluctance to move.

'You said something about her legs,' Sister reminded her as she entered. Pippa told her what she'd found. Julian nodded.

'She's her own worst enemy,' he said. 'She complains about the things that aren't important, and ignores the ones that are.'

'Did you finish the recordings, Nurse Garland?' asked Sister.

I'm sorry, Sister, I only did that room. Mrs Yates was feeling upset, so I talked to her, then Mrs Warner's legs—Shall I—?'

'I'll get someone else to do them. I want you to help over on the AN side. Staff Midwife Smith is all alone, and she's got a suspected premature labour.'

As Pippa left, conscious of Julian's gaze on her back, she heard him asking Sister to contact Mr Warner, to warn him of the severity of his wife's condition.

It was but a short walk along the corridor towards the antenatal side, but all the way she was thinking of Julian and the way he'd looked at her while she told them about Mrs Warner's leg. It had taken all her will-power to resist the pull of those gorgeous blue eyes. Her pulses were still racing.

By the time she'd wandered round the rooms on AN, looking for Staff Midwife Smith, and found her, she'd calmed down. Lorna Smith was with an anxious-looking girl in one of the four-bedded rooms, fiddling with the drip, and trying to reassure the girl that the drug was usually quite efficient at stopping labour. She gave a sigh of relief when she saw Pippa enter.

'Thank God. This has really held us up, and the recordings haven't been done, and Mrs Carby's got a headache, so you'd better check her blood-pressure thoroughly. Got that?'

'Sure.' As she turned to go, a bell rang. Then again.

'That'll be Mrs Munro in the side ward,' said Nurse Smith. 'She's a new patient. Hyperemesis. She's probably been sick again.'

Pippa hurried along to the single room showing a red light over the door, and went inside.

'I've been sick again,' came a plaintive voice from the bed, and Pippa saw a pretty girl with long, copper-coloured hair, hugging a vomit bowl to her expensive embroidered nightdress. She hastened to take it, and the girl lay exhausted against the pillows.

'Would you like a wash?' Mrs Carby would

205

just have to wait a minute.

'I'd love one. But I feel so weak.'

'I'll do it.'

When it was done, and she smelled fresh and clean again, Mrs Munro smiled gratefully at Pippa.

'You nurses are so kind,' she said breathily. 'I know I couldn't do such a job. I'm an actress.'

'I thought your face was familiar,' said Pippa tactfully, although she was sure she'd never seen the girl before.

'I've been on television. That's where I met my husband.'

'Is he an actor?'

'He's Felix Munro! He's a famous film director. You must have heard of him.'

'Oh—yes—of course!' She hadn't.

'It doesn't matter. He's walked out on me.'

'I don't believe it! Does he know you're pregnant?'

'Of course he does. He's gone off with Lisa Carlton. They've been seen together.'

Pippa had heard of Lisa Carlton. Everyone had heard of Lisa Carlton. Married four times, her name had been romantically linked with most of the leading film actors.

'That was very cruel of him.'

'You don't have to feel sorry for me. I'm not alone. I was engaged to someone else before I met Felix, and he's come back into my life. When my divorce is settled, I expect we shall marry.'

Pippa had her back to the girl, reading her latest recordings. It was just as she'd registered the girl's first name—Olivia—and a warning note had sounded in her brain, that the girl said, in a bright, little-girlish voice, 'I expect you've met him. He's a doctor here. His name's Julian Reed.'

CHAPTER TWELVE

As if from a distance, Pippa heard Olivia's light laugh. All she could feel was her heart beating remorselessly on in her chest. Yet she was sure she was dead. Or dreaming.

'Dr Reed?' she echoed, reluctantly turning to face Olivia.

'You've met him? I believe he's quite new here.'

'Yes, I've met him.'

'Then you may have heard of me. I'm Olivia. We wcre going to be married last year, but he was always being called away. Every party, every evening out, he'd be called to some emergency, some woman going into labour, or needing an operation. I hardly ever saw him. And then I met Felix, and he swept me off my feet.'

'So you didn't love Julian.' Was she grasping at straws?

'Of course I loved him.' Her voice dropped. 'I still do.'

'But you're married now, you're having a baby.'

'That doesn't stop me loving him.'

'He may have changed his feelings towards you,' said Pippa desperately.

'I know he hasn't. He's told me.'

A heavy stone settled in Pippa's stomach. 'You gave him up because he was always being called away,' Pippa insisted. 'He is still called away. Frequently.'

'At the moment,' said Olivia stubbornly. 'But he's going to be a consultant soon. He told me only the other day. Consultants don't get called out. Well, not very often.'

Pippa took a deep breath. 'But you're having a baby, and it isn't his. You can't expect—'

'Who says it isn't? Oh, God, I feel sick again!' She grabbed at a disposable bowl and retched into it. Conflicting emotions churning around inside her, and an awful sick feeling in the pit of her stomach, Pippa automatically wiped Olivia's face and took away the bowl.

'I should never have given him up,' said Olivia reflectively. 'He realises that, too. I half suspected he'd have found someone else, but he says he hasn't.' At that Pippa felt a wrench in her heart. Olivia went blithely on. 'When he came to see me yesterday afternoon, and I was being sick everywhere, he was so attentive, so worried about me. He didn't stay long, but he made sure he got me in here straight away.'

Julian had arranged her admission! Pippa swallowed. And he'd been to see her yesterday afternoon? But he'd been with her—except for the half an hour when he'd been into Petersfield to buy a birthday card. Now it all fitted! The friend in Petersfield was Olivia! And he must have been on his way to see her when Pippa's car broke down. Yet all the while . . . And all the things he'd said to her—he hadn't meant them at all! Keeping her voice calm, she said to Olivia, 'You came in yesterday afternoon?'

'Oh, no, not then. He came back in the evening and arranged all that.' Pippa nodded. When he'd left her at Harvey's Garage, she'd mentioned something about going to the cinema that evening, and he'd said he'd love to take her but he was on call. On call! Well, she wouldn't be asking him again. And a desperate sadness seemed to overwhelm her. Olivia was chattering happily.

'Julian said I had to come in. He said he wanted me where he could keep an eye on me.' She giggled. 'Well, I knew what he meant by that! Naughty man!' She picked up a glossy magazine.

Her heart breaking, Pippa collected the bowls and took them out to the sluice. She rested her face against the cold tiles of the wall, and allowed herself the luxury of tears.

Of course, she should have known. He'd never actually said he loved her. And she'd never said she loved him. But surely it must have showed? Had she been deceived by his deep blue gaze and gentle touch? At the thought of that kiss in the car her skin felt hot and her knees began to shake. How could she have shown her feelings so transparently? What a fool she had been! He had used her, he had been aware of her feelings for him, and he had taken advantage of them. How could he have said all those things to her? She could hear his voice saying them as if he were there.

'I thought it only made you look even more adorable.' 'I shall really come and put you to bed. Is there room for me?' And how foolishly she had let her feelings show then. 'There's always room for you.'

Then, going to her mother's in the car, what had he said? 'You won't ever hurt me, will you, Pippa?'

Look how he'd hurt her! Didn't he care? She shivered, and a sob rose in her throat. Why hadn't she listened to her mother?

More of his words came unbidden to her mind. 'You are too kind, and too gentle, and far too vulnerable. You need someone to protect you.' She'd thought he'd been offering his services! And then he'd kissed her. A magical, wonderful kiss that she could still feel on her lips now. She clenched her fists. She would not cry over him!

'Can you give Mrs Fryer a bedpan, Nurse Garland?' came Nurse Smith's voice from outside the sluice. Pippa jumped up, and grabbed one from the rack, inserting a disposable one at the same time.

'Yes, Staff.'

'She's on complete bed rest. Pre-eclampsia,' said Lorna Smith as Pippa emerged. 'How is Mrs Munro?'

'Oh—she's fine!'

Pippa rushed out into the ward, without first checking where Mrs Fryer was situated, and Nurse Smith watched her with a puzzled frown.

'She's in B,' she called out. Pippa paused, nodded.

'Oh. Yes.' And she disappeared into one of the four-bedded rooms. She had forced a bright smile to her face, and Mrs Fryer remarked, as Pippa drew the curtains, 'You look happy, Nurse!'

'Oh, yes, Mrs Fryer. I'm always happy.'

'Nice to see a smiling face.'

Pippa set the bedpan beneath her and hurried from the ward. There was only one thing for it. She had to immerse herself in her work, she had to deliberately take her mind off Julian Reed and his false words. She had to forget how he'd kissed her, she'd have to forget the way he'd often looked at her, with love in those lapis lazuli eyes. Of course, it hadn't been love. She'd read into them what she'd wanted to see. It hadn't been love at all. Pity?

Angrily, she fetched the sphygmo-manometer and started round the patients, checking them, and all the while keeping a determined smile on her face.

When Pippa returned from coffee at half-past nine, relieved that she hadn't met anyone and been obliged to talk, Felicity White called her into the office. For a moment, Pippa wondered if she'd upset someone on the AN side, and they'd made a complaint. But Sister White was smiling.

'When do you take your finals, Nurse Garland?'

'September, Sister.'

'That's only a few weeks away. I think it's about time you took some responsibility. You did staff for a while after you qualified in general?'

'For a year, Sister.'

'Then it won't be too strange for you. I'd like you to be Acting Staff Midwife on the antenatal side when Nurse Smith is off duty.'

'Oh.' The first thing that came into her mind was Olivia. She'd have to talk to her, look after her, and she'd be bound to see Julian.

'Aren't you pleased about it?' asked Sister, watching her.

'Oh, yes. It's a great opportunity,' she gabbled. Who cared that her heart was breaking? Come to that, who even knew? She'd just have to learn how to keep a smile on her face, and hope it didn't look too much like a grimace. And, in time, perhaps the hurt would go away.

'Bearing in mind,' Sister went on, 'that it's only while Staff Midwife Simpson is off sick, and I'd rather keep Nurse Waters over here. But it will be excellent experience for you, particularly if you intend to stay on. I mean— just for a short while. I expect—are you still going out to Chile?'

Still? For a moment Pippa almost wished she were, to get away from Julian and Olivia. Did Sister White know anything?

'No, Sister. I'm not going to Chile.'

Sister's face cleared. 'So you'll be staying on. The PNO will be pleased. She doesn't ask everyone to stay on, you know, but she did mention your name—perhaps I'm talking out of turn.'

'That's all right, Sister.'

'Are you all right, Nurse? You look upset. I expect I've put my foot in it, haven't I, talking about Chile? I expect you were anxious to be married and going out there. I'm sorry, I did hear about it. It must have been very upsetting for you, and it will take a while to get over it.'

She smiled sympathetically. Pippa tried to respond. Did Sister really think she was feeling upset over Neil? She had been upset, true, but it had been quickly followed by relief.

'Sister, you've got it—' An idea occurred to her. 'Yes, it was very upsetting, Sister. But I shall get over it.' She smiled bravely. Yes, let them think she was miserable and irritable because of the broken engagement. Then she wouldn't have to put on a face all the time. Never, never, let them know who she really grieved for.

'If you go along to AN now,' said Sister, obviously relieved that the awkward conversation was over, 'Nurse Smith will tell you all about the patients. It's a good introduction to responsibility, antenatal care. And it's not quite as strenuous as delivery and postnatal.'

Pippa collected her bag and cloak and put them in a locker on the AN side. She found Lorna Smith talking to Olivia, and the Staff Midwife immediately came out to her.

'Back from coffee? Good, then I can go. You're staying?'

Pippa told her what Sister had said and Nurse Smith's eyes gleamed behind her glasses. 'Right, then I'll tell you all about them. Come into the office.' She quickly read through the Kardex. Most of the patients were fairly straightforward cases, pre-eclamptic toxaemias, threatened miscarriages, suspected placenta praevias, and multiple pregnancies.

'A few problems,' said Lorna, pulling a face. 'Not bad ones. We've got a couple of postnatal patients who came in when the PN side was full. They're in singles. There's Sally Hobson, very young, not married. She had a really terrible forceps delivery, don't know how it happened, she's just one of those people that these things seem to happen to. And they weren't too sure that the baby was all right. He really went through the mill, poor little chap. They can't find anything wrong, but he seems to cry a lot. Probably Sally's attitude. She seems to resent him sometimes. Can't say I blame her.'

'Poor kid,' murmured Pippa.

'It is a shame. Then there's Mrs Munro opposite. She's not one of the overflow, of course. But you've met her, haven't you? I'd better tell you more about her.'

I know enough, thought Pippa. But she put a fixed smile on her face and listened.

'It's her first baby, fourteen weeks, but her morning sickness never seemed to disappear, and lately has even become worse. Dr Reed brought her in last night. I believe he's acquainted with her.'

One way of putting it, thought Pippa.

'We are inclined to think it's psychosomatic. Her husband hasn't been to see her yet, and she's told everyone conflicting stories about him.'

'She told me he'd left her,' said Pippa.

'That's one version. We really don't know the truth. She seems very immature. But then, she's an actress.'

A shaft of hope shot through Pippa. Could it not be true then? Was it all a fiction?

'We're getting Dr Winter the psychiatrist to see her tomorrow. He's really more into puerperal psychosis, I believe, rejection of the baby and all that. I suppose this could be similar, in a way.'

Rejecting the baby, thought Pippa. Because it was Julian's? Perhaps she knew she couldn't marry Julian, so she felt guilty about his baby?

'Guilt,' she remarked, without thinking. Lorna Smith looked surprised.

'Yes, I suppose you could be right. I hadn't really thought about it, but I'm not very well up in psychiatry. Now, the other one from PN is Cathy Pole. She's a rhesus patient who slipped through the net a few years ago, so she didn't get her anti-D after her first baby. She was abroad, I think. Her second baby was badly affected by the antibodies, had an exchange transfusion at birth. She lost the next one at thirty-four weeks, after intrauterine transfusions. And she's just lost another at thirty-two weeks.'

'Oh, that's unbelievable!' breathed Pippa.

'It is, these days. The transfusions sometimes work, but not always. She's feeling pretty low, but she's putting on a brave face. I haven't seen her cry yet. It would do her good.'

'It's difficult to know what to say to these women who have lost their babies,' said Pippa. 'So easy to fall back on platitudes.' Lorna nodded.

'The only other one you'll need to watch is Mrs Jarvis. She's the young kid who started contractions this morning. She's got an incompetent cervix, with a Shirodkar suture. She's lost three babies, all around five months. She's thirty-three weeks now, but she's having a few twinges. We've sedated her, given her something we hope will stop it. Dr Reed seems to think she'll be OK. He'd like her to last to thirty-six weeks if she can. It's a smallish baby. If she starts in earnest you must send for him immediately. She'll have to go to theatre to have the suture removed.'

'I understand.'

'I shan't be coming back after coffee, Nurse Garland. I'm giving a lecture to antenatal mums.'

'I thought the health visitors did those.'

'They do. But I've decided to become a midwifery tutor, so I feel I ought to have a go. That's why I'm trying it out on the antenatal mums. They won't be as critical as the students!' She laughed. 'Sister will probably send you the auxiliary in a while.' She picked up her cloak and left the ward.

Pippa had a brief feeling of importance. She was in charge of the ward; well, the AN side, at least. She read quickly through the report and rapidly became deflated. There was such a lot to know. She knew she wasn't as confident as she looked, but the patients wouldn't know she'd never been in charge before.

She decided to visit Cathy Pole first. Her experience had touched her heart-strings. She hoped she'd be able to do something to help.

The woman was lying with her eyes closed. She had a sort of fragile prettiness, although there were dark shadows under her eyes as though she hadn't slept. Was she sleeping now? Pippa started to tiptoe out.

'Did you want me, Nurse?' The voice was soft and cultured. Pippa turned back.

'I'm sorry if I woke you.'

'I wasn't asleep. I don't sleep very well. They have to drug me to the eyeballs.' She attempted a smile, but her brown eyes were full of misery. At that moment Pippa felt she understood. She didn't say anything, just went and sat on the bed and put her hand on Cathy's. Their eyes met for a brief moment, then Cathy's mouth trembled, and her eyes filled with tears. Pippa put her arms around her.

'Oh, God,' whispered Cathy, as the tears slid down her pale cheeks. 'Why did it have to be me? Wasn't once enough?'

Pippa held the woman's slender body, as violent sobs racked her. Pippa's throat was hurting, too, and she had to fight back her own tears. It wasn't her place to cry. She had to be the strong one. So she swallowed hard, and forced the tears back, and tried to think of something happy, as she patted Cathy's shoulders and made soothing noises.

It seemed to be ages before Cathy stopped crying, and gently withdrew from Pippa's sympathetic hug. She blew her nose and dabbed her eyes.

'I'm sorry. I didn't mean to do that. It just— sort of came. It's strange, you know. I feel I've been living a dream, a nightmare. I couldn't believe what had happened. They all talked to me, reassured me, made excuses for me. But I couldn't believe them. I knew I couldn't have lost the baby. He had to be in the special unit somewhere. That sort of thing doesn't happen twice. Do you understand?'

Pippa nodded. She did understand. She'd felt like that when her father had died. She felt part of her was missing. She hadn't known him, so she couldn't believe he was dead. Yet somehow she missed him. And Cathy hadn't really known, had never seen her baby. Yet she . . .

'When you came into the room, I thought, here it comes again, and I waited for the platitudes. But you didn't say anything, just came and touched me. And suddenly it was all real, it had really happened. I couldn't cry before because it wasn't true. I must have bottled it all up.' She sighed and smiled tremulously. 'I shall have to start over again, shan't I, and pick up the pieces? I have to grieve, don't I?'

'Yes, Cathy. You have to grieve.'

'Do you mind if I talk a bit? I feel like talking.'

'Talk away.' Never mind the other patients. This was important.

'I didn't think it could happen again. I thought this time it would all work out. The other baby I lost was a girl, and I already have two daughters. I still minded terribly when it happened. But I really wanted a boy, not for my sake, but for Jeffrey's. He's been married before, you see, and has got another daughter. I was sure we'd have a boy one day. And the doctors encouraged me.'

She paused and blew her nose.

'I had a fifty-fifty chance of having a rhesus negative baby, they said. So we decided to try again. And it was rhesus positive.'

'You were very brave even to consider it,' said Pippa, holding her hand.

'Well, it was—hoping for a boy, you see. It was a boy.'

'How do you feel about trying again?' asked Pippa.

'It's too early to try to make a decision like that,' said Cathy.

'Of course it is. It was insensitive of me to suggest it.'

'I suppose—if I did get pregnant again, well, I'd have to give it the chance of life, wouldn't I?'

'Oh, Cathy, I've never met anyone as brave as you.'

'No,' said Cathy gently. 'The bravery is yet to come, when I have to tell the girls they haven't got their baby brother after all.'

Pippa's throat contracted painfully. Tears were suddenly near the surface. She squeezed Cathy's hand, and rushed from the room, her eyes so misted over that she collided with a tall figure in white.

'Hey—hey—'

He held her firmly, and she collapsed against him, the tears falling unchecked.

'It's not fair, it's not fair!' she wept. 'Why should she have to suffer like that, when she's done nothing wrong to anyone? She's a lovely mother, I can tell, and there's others, horrible, wicked people, and nothing goes wrong for them, and they have as many children as they want, and half the time they don't want them, either, and they abuse them, and batter them, and neglect them, and Cathy, she's so sweet, yet the baby died—It's not fair, Julian! It's just not fair! I don't think there's a God. He wouldn't do things like that!'

Her eyes bright, her lips trembling, she looked up at him. It had seemed so natural to fall into his arms, to feel her body stirring at his touch. Sudden memory made her jerk back, away from him. He looked puzzled.

'I'm sorry, forgive me, I didn't mean to do that, I was just upset.'

'You are upset. Come and sit down.' He took her arm, leading her towards the office.

'I'm all right now—'

'Do as you're told.' He spoke firmly.

She sat down by the desk, and he sat a couple of feet away, looking at her. Already her treacherous heart was thudding at his nearness. Be quiet, heart, she told herself. He means nothing to you. He's marrying Olivia. Or—so she said! Hope started to rise in her, and her cheeks flushed under his scrutiny.

'It's Cathy Pole, isn't it?'

She nodded. 'Oh, Juilan, it's so tragic, I did so want to help her—but she was crying so, I think her heart is breaking—'

'She's crying? But that's marvellous, Pippa! You have helped her. She's started to grieve, that's part of the healing process. She's got to go through it, or go under.'

'But it's not fair, Julian! It's not fair at all!'

'Life isn't fair, Pippa. We can't always have what we want.'

His voice sounded sad. Was he thinking of Olivia? Had she told the truth—she wanted to marry him, but couldn't? Was that the true situation? Pippa bit her lip. Her heart was pounding in anticipation of what she must ask him. She'd tried not to mention Olivia to him before, but now she must. 'Julian, I've been talking to Olivia.'

He nodded. 'Is she still vomiting?' The question was professional and impersonal. Was he hiding his true feelings for the girl?

'Yes, she is. Julian, she—'

'It's got to be psychological. Felix has been filming in France. He should have returned last week but he didn't. According to Olivia, he just made lame excuses. Then an actress friend—some friend!—said he'd been seen with a famous film star.'

'Lisa Carlton,' said Pippa. So that had been true. Had it all been true?

'She told you? Well, on the surface things do look bad, but I know Felix. He adores Olivia, he wouldn't walk out on her at a time like this. He's forty-eight, but it's his first baby. He's over the moon.'

'But Olivia doesn't seem to care if he's gone, Julian. She said—'

'Of course she cares. She idolises him.' He frowned, then his expression lightened. 'I get the picture. She's been embroidering the facts again. She's an actress, Pippa. A bit of the hysteric in her, as in most actors and actresses. She does it for attention.'

So was any of it true? Pippa felt joy welling up in her until she thought she'd burst.

'So you're not going to marry her?'

'Marry Olivia? She's already married. My silly, silly Pippa, why would I want to marry Olivia when I've got you? Olivia is very sweet, I'm very fond of her, but she's dreadfully immature, and awfully self-centred. That's why she's good at her job.'

'She said you'd come back into her life,' said Pippa jerkily. 'She said she should never have let you go. She said you couldn't bear to let her out of your sight. And she—'

Julian leaned forward and laid a finger on her lips.

'I don't want to hear any more about Olivia. Come here.'

She got up and went to him, and his arms went around her. His lips came down on hers, firm and demanding. She closed her eyes and waited for the ecstasy she knew would come.

In the ward, a bell rang. 'Damn,' murmured Julian, letting her go. He had an unfathomable expression in his eyes. 'You'd better answer that,' he suggested. 'It might be Mrs Jarvis going into labour.'

Pippa's eyes widened in alarm, and she hurried into the ward. But it was just Mrs Fryer wanting another bedpan. And when she came back to the office, the door was wide open, and the room was empty.

By the time Pippa had done all the morning tasks, giving out drugs and taking more recordings, it was almost lunchtime. She had a split shift, which meant having the afternoon off, and she had planned to go into Basingstoke to look at the red Astra. If it was still there. It had been there when she'd gone past yesterday. Yesterday. It seemed such an age ago.

Sister had sent the auxiliary from the PN side, Mrs Dexter, and she had dealt with the more menial tasks; bedpans, drinks, and

Olivia's vomit bowls.

'She's very quiet, isn't she?' said Mrs Dexter, after she'd given out clean jugs and glasses.

'Who—Mrs Munro?'

'No, that other one, in the single opposite. The baby that cries such a lot. It's crying now.'

'Why doesn't she pick it up and cuddle it?' wondered Pippa.

'Perhaps she's one of those who believe babies shouldn't be picked up all the time in case they get spoiled. I must say, I didn't take any notice of that sort of thing, and my five are all happy kids. Mind you, they're grown up now. The youngest's fourteen.'

Pippa sensed she would go on for ever, so she tactfully said, 'I thought that idea had gone a long time ago. I'd better go and check.'

She had ten minutes before lunch; Sister had said, not long ago when she'd come round to see if Pippa was all right, that Staff Midwife Smith would be back by lunchtime.

Pippa pushed open the door of the single room and went inside. The baby in the crib by the window was crying in fits and starts, as if he'd given up hope of anyone attending to him. Sally Hobson, a young, round-faced girl with light brown hair and owlish spectacles, lay in bed, her gaze fixed on the ceiling.

'What's the matter with him?' asked Pippa, crossing to the crib and lifting out the baby. His little face was puckered and red, his skin damp with sweat. His cries subsided as she rocked him against her shoulder. Sally had turned her head and was gazing at the scene.

'Did you wind him?' asked Pippa.

'Oh, yes. I always wind him.' Her tone was flat and bored.

'Did you change him?'

'Of course I changed him.' Now she sounded cross.

'Well, he's soaking wet. I'll get you another nappy.'

She placed the baby in the crib while she bent and opened the little cupboard underneath it, where nappies were kept. There was a pile of clean ones on the bottom shelf. As Pippa took one she felt something cold and hard tucked between them. She thrust in her hand, and pulled out an almost full bottle of baby milk.

Staring at it in amazement, she held it out to Sally. 'What's this?'

'His ten o'clock feed.' She spoke nonchalantly.

'But he's only had about an ounce! Why did you tell me he'd had four ounces?'

'I forgot. I got mixed up with yesterday. He didn't want it today. He wasn't hungry.'

'He sounds hungry now,' said Pippa, as the baby started to cry again. 'Look, you change his nappy while I warm his feed.'

'I don't feel up to it. I'm tired.'

Pippa gave her a searching look and

changed the baby's nappy herself. She put the baby in his crib and took the lid off the bucket to put in the soiled nappy. At the bottom of the empty bucket sat three potatoes, two slices of meat, and a handful of peas. Horrified, she glanced up at Sally who was muttering to herself.

'Aren't you sleeping, Sally?' she asked.

'No,' said the girl without turning.

'How's your appetite?'

'Can't be bothered. I never eat much.'

'Would you like to hold the baby while I fetch the feed?'

'No. Leave me alone. He cries too much. He hates me.' All the words had been delivered in a flat monotone. Pippa forced a smile to her face.

'I think I'll take him across to the nursery to feed him,' she said lightly.

'As you wish.'

Relieved that Sally hadn't objected, Pippa wheeled the crib out of the room. Puerperal psychosis was the tentative diagnosis she had made, and if she were right, something had to be done quickly. She'd have to tell someone. And the baby would have to be kept in the nursery until help came.

Who should she tell? Julian had left the ward some time ago. Sister White should be over on the PN side. Could she leave the ward in Mrs Dexter's hands for a moment? The nursery was over there, anyway. She started to

227

wheel the crib past Olivia's room. The door was half open, and she casually glanced in. Her breath caught in her throat.

She'd know that back, those shoulders, that head, anywhere. She knew how those arms felt when they were holding her close. So how could he do this to her? And after all he'd said!

Her feet seemed to be glued to the floor, her eyes fixed on the scene inside the room. Julian had his back to her, as he sat on the side of the bed, his arms around Olivia, his face bent into her neck. Olivia's pale arms were round his neck, her eyes closed as he spoke to her in a soft voice.

It seemed to Pippa that the whole hospital, the whole world, had come to a halt. There was a deathly silence everywhere, so that Olivia's clear, actress's voice carried across the room towards her.

'Oh, Julian, you don't know how I've been waiting for you. I thought you were never coming. Julian, tell me again what you just told me. Tell me so I can really believe you.'

They parted slightly, and Pippa could see they were looking deeply into each other's eyes. She had a lump in her throat, and could hardly breathe.

'I told everyone about it, Julian. I knew it would happen. Oh, you can't possibly know how happy you've made me!'

Stifling the sobs in her throat, Pippa almost

228

ran with the crib over to the PN side. Struggling to keep control, she said breathlessly to Sister White, 'I've brought Sally Hobson's baby. She's got puerperal psychosis, and she's thrown her lunch in the bin—'

Sister White was looking most puzzled and concerned. 'Will you say that again, Nurse Garland?'

When she got back to AN, Julian had gone, and Olivia lay in her pretty pink finery, a smile on her face, like a cat that had got the cream. Lorna Smith had just arrived, and was wondering where Pippa had got to. Mrs Dexter seemed as puzzled as she was.

'She was here a minute ago, Nurse Smith. She went to see Sally Hobson's baby. It was crying again.'

At that moment Pippa pushed through the glass doors, and they turned towards her.

'You left the ward unattended, Nurse Garland,' said Lorna accusingly, and her grey eyes flashed behind her glasses.

Pippa was having difficulty in focusing her attention on what she was saying.

'I'm sorry—I took Sally's baby over to the nursery—'

'What's wrong with her?'

So Pippa had to explain all over again, more calmly than last time. Lorna's expression softened.

'I think you should have told Mrs Dexter where you were going, in case of emergency.

But you're right, it does sound as if she's developing puerperal psychosis. I'll get Dr Winters. And while he's here he can take a look at Mrs Munro.'

'She's looking more cheerful,' Pippa couldn't resist saying. Like a little pink cat, she was thinking, then felt guilty.

'You'd better go to lunch,' said Nurse Smith. 'Have you filled in the Kardex?'

'Yes. Oh—how did the talk go?'

Lorna Smith grimaced. 'I'm going to need a lot of practice!'

*   *   *

Pippa didn't feel like lunch. She didn't feel like anything, except desperate. She knew she couldn't talk to people, putting on a brave face, pretending everything was all right. Living a lie was not her style. And at once she was glad she'd told no one how she felt about Julian. The last thing she wanted right now was pity.

She ran up to her flat and let herself inside. It was empty. Over the back of a chair in the kitchen, her beige jacket lay where she'd tossed it. Julian had put this jacket round her shoulders. She shivered as she recalled that moment. That was the night he'd found her crying and taken her to the wine bar. That was the night he'd kissed her. Really kissed her. Foolishly, she'd thought he loved her, too. But

230

he had never said he loved her. Not in those words. Not 'I love you, Pippa.'

So it was all her fault for reading into his actions feeilngs he didn't have. Yet—and his words today came into her mind. 'Why would I have to marry Olivia when I've got you?' Well, he'd certainly had her where he wanted—on the end of a string! But no more. He could say what he wanted now, she'd never believe him again!

She banged her fist on the table. Damn the man! She'd given up Neil. She'd lost Julian. Had he ever been hers? She jumped up angrily. She knew what she'd do. She'd go into Basingstoke and she'd buy the red Astra. Yes, damn him. She wasn't going to sit and mope over him.

She changed her clothes and ran down to the car park. As she started to move the car away, a figure came down the steps towards a cream Rover. Gritting her teeth, she put her foot on the accelerator, and missed him by inches as she roared away. Through the mirror she could see his amazed expression, and she laughed. That would teach him to treat her like that!

She reached the garage, and got out. The red Astra had been over here, next to the green Montego. But next to the green Montego was a yellow Renault. Her heart sank. This just wasn't her day, and she fought to keep back the tears of frustration.

'Can I help you, madam?'

'Oh—no—it doesn't matter—'

'Is it the Montego you like? It's a lovely little car, only done—'

'No, it was—well, I saw a red Astra here yesterday. I took a fancy to it.'

'The Astra? Went this morning. It's over in the other bay.'

She gave a rueful smile. 'It doesn't matter.' She turned to go.

'It wouldn't have gone with your hair,' said the salesman. He was young, with impudent eyes and an arrogant swing to his hips in their tight blue jeans.

Pippa's temper rose. 'I shall have a red car if I want to,' she said angrily. 'Anyway—'

'Nice white Cavalier just along here. That would match your hair.' Another one taking exception to her hair! Was there no end to them?

'No, thank you.'

'And here's a lovely little Mini. Cream's such a fashionable colour. Looks smart.'

'I'm sure it does.' Cream, like a Rover she knew. That would be worse than anything. That cream Rover was going to be around for a long time. She'd probably see it every day, see him every day. A gleam came into her eye. It was Fate. The car had gone. Julian had gone. There was just one thing to do.

She flashed a smile at the brash salesman. 'No, I don't think I'll have a car at the moment. You see, I shall be going abroad to work very soon.'

'Lucky you.'

'Yes. I shall be going to Australia.'

CHAPTER THIRTEEN

Every little sound echoed in the big room. Someone coughed. Someone turned a paper. A pen rolled on a desk.

Pippa glanced at her watch. Twenty minutes to go. She was halfway through the last question. She read it again.

'Write short notes on four of the following:-
a) Foetal distress.' She'd chosen that, of course, remembering Gail Carey who'd had a Caesarean. She remembered watching Julian's strong, gentle hands as he skilfully extracted the distressed baby. Not too distressed, fortunately. She remembered daydreaming during the operation, and Julian's impatience while they waited for her to count the swabs. Her face grew hot as she thought of it, and she was aware of Sister Tutor watching her.

She quickly read through her second answer. 'b) Diabetes.' Another obvious one for her. Joan—what was her name? Green, or something like it. Ten pounder, that baby, but it still had to go down to SCBU, because it was premature. It hadn't stayed long.

She'd taken it down herself, and Neil had been there, and he'd kissed her, and Julian had seen it. Neil had gone back to Chile without contacting Pippa. She knew then how deeply he must have been hurt, and she hated herself. At the same time she almost envied him the way he'd apparently got over his disappointment. Her information about him had, of course, come from Lucy, who had seen him a few times before he left the country. He'd taken her home, and this time, it seemed, his father had met her and taken a liking to her. Just lately she'd been dropping a few hints about Chile, and Pippa had glimpsed a library book on the subject, and a Spanish phrase book.

Neil had written to Lucy, but not one word about Pippa, and she felt mortified. She had hoped they could remain friends. Perhaps one day, when he was married—to Lucy?—he'd realise she'd done the right thing.

Sighing, she turned back to her question paper. 'c) Abnormal presentation.'

A long question, this, but she'd chosen it because of Sara, and her baby who had arrived face first. She recalled the delivery as if it were yesterday, the way the amniotic membrane wouldn't break, the way the cord was twice around the neck—a surge of indignation swept over her as she remembered Julian's crossness and impatience, and later, after his apology, his angry kiss.

She wrote quickly all she could remember about the delivery of Sara's baby. Now she had to choose one more question from the remaining three. 'd) rhesus incompatibility. e) puerperal psychosis. f) eclampsia.'

Each one had connotations for her. The first one reminded her of Cathy, who had lost her baby. Pippa had cried desperately, and Julian had held her in his arms. And he'd told her all about Olivia, and how he wasn't in love with her, and she'd believed him. She bit her lip, trying to stem the painful memories.

The second one—ah, that was Sally Hobson, who had worried her so, sent her running out of the ward, past Olivia's room. Pippa hadn't been around when Olivia had been discharged, a few days later. She'd been sent down to Ward Two, where the staff situation was desperate. There'd been no further mention of her carrying on as Acting Staff Midwife on Six. She knew it had to be because she'd almost lost control after finding Julian and Olivia in each other's arms. Sister hadn't known about that, of course. She thought she was upset about Sally Hobson. Sally had been sent to a psychiatric hospital, and, fortunately, her mother had been only too anxious to look after the baby.

Next day the Senior Nursing Officer had made arrangements for a bank midwife to take over the AN side, and Pippa hadn't seen Olivia again.

She glanced at her watch, and fought down rising panic. Only ten minutes left, and she still had to choose one of the last three questions. She'd have to stop this daydreaming lark. Well, it had to be the last one. Eclampsia. She'd already read a lot about it, even before she'd looked after Diane Emery. Yes, she'd write about Diane—but she couldn't do that without recalling every moment of that eventful day.

The new senior registrar had turned out to be the man who had humiliated her at Heathrow, the one with the vivid blue eyes. But he hadn't been the arrogant man she'd thought him to be, and his voice had made her knees go weak. He'd stood close to her as she took Diane's blood-pressure, and her heart had raced. In fact, it had hardly slowed down since!

But still he couldn't refrain from teasing her about dropping things, and referring to her red hair. It wasn't her fault she looked like Olivia. It didn't make her love him any the less.

He'd saved Diane, and he'd saved the baby. And he'd taken her heart. But she had solved her problem. She had applied to three hospitals in Melbourne, where one of her cousins had emigrated to. It seemed there was every chance she'd get a job. And, sure enough, a reply had come from one of them, offering her a post of midwife, initially on a two-year contract. Two years should be long enough, she decided, to forget Julian Reed.

Today, in her pocket, was a letter to Melbourne. A letter of acceptance. Her mother had been rather upset, and hadn't understood Pippa's reasons for going. She still thought it was Neil, and Pippa was regretting her action. And Pippa let her think so. She hated denying Julian, it made her feel like Peter in the Bible. Eleanor had grumbled about how she was going to miss Pippa, but Pippa had pointed out she'd have leave, and she'd be able to come home, as Neil had.

The seconds were ticking by.

'Five minutes,' said Sister Tutor, in a clear voice. There was a rattling of paper, a shuffling of feet and chairs. Pippa wrote rapidly, trying to remember all she could of Diane's traumatic day in Room Three.

After it was all over, and the baby safely delivered and taken to SCBU, he had rushed away and left the notes behind. She'd taken them and he'd closed the door, and there'd been just the two of them in the room, closeted together. Her heart started to thud at the memory. She mustn't think of him, she had to forget him!

Her hand flew over the paper.

He had put his hands on her shoulders, she had felt the strength of them through the thin fabric of her dress. What had he said? She knew she would never forget it.

'My God, your eyes really are green!'

So were Olivia's. He really did have a 'thing'

about red hair and green eyes, didn't he? Well, he could indulge his weakness every day, now he had Olivia again.

'Pens down.'

Pippa scribbled the last few words and laid down her pen with a sigh. She glanced around her, exchanged a grimace with Debbie Page. It was all over. Two written papers, and just the viva to come. If she failed, there could be no going out to Australia. She'd have to stay here, to resit it, stay here and see Julian every day.

She collected her things and got up. A babble of voices filled the room, as the girls exchanged comments about the paper. Some were complaining that you didn't see rhesus incompatibility these days. How could you write about it? Pippa casually mentioned Cathy Pole, and the others were amazed. They went eagerly along the corridor towards the lifts.

With the summer flu laying off so many staff, Pippa had been moving from ward to ward, to make up numbers. She had seen very little of Julian, except from a distance. And, of course, when she was on Ward Two, she didn't see him at all. His firm had beds on Four, Five and Six. She had only heard that Olivia had gone home from a colleague. Had Julian moved in with her, to comfort her after losing Felix?

And now they had put her on Outpatients from today. She had no idea how long she'd be working there. Could be days, could be until she left the hospital next January. She could hardly wait for that day to come.

She went down to the dining-room for lunch. She found herself sitting next to Debbie, who talked non-stop about her three-year-old son, William. Pippa was relieved when she eventually left, to make an urgent phone call home.

'I hope it's not measles,' she wailed, as she left. Pippa fetched a coffee and went across to an empty alcove to drink it. Lost in her thoughts of the written paper, and imagining what the viva might be like, she was only mildly disturbed when someone came and sat opposite. She took a sip of coffee and looked up. And almost dropped the cup. Julian was watching her with a pained expression in his eyes. For a moment she couldn't draw away. Then she tightened her lips, and tried to ignore the way her heart was behaving. She put down her cup and started to rise.

'You haven't finished your coffee.' His voice was low and intimate. She shivered.

'I have to get back.'

'You've only been here twenty minutes. Why are you avoiding me?'

'I'm sorry. I don't feel like talking. I've had a traumatic morning.'

'How come?' Did he know the effect his voice had on her?

'The second written paper.' And all the time

239

it reminded me of you.

'Good questions?' he asked. Pippa could have sworn he really cared, but of course, he was just being polite. He was always polite.

'Not too bad. Fortunately, most of the questions dealt with problems I've met in patients.'

'That must have been heaven-sent.' She wished he wouldn't look at her like that, those blue eyes so intense, that faint amused smile on his face.

'Certainly useful.'

'Eclampsia, I suppose? Face presentation? Multiple pregnancy?' He raised an eyebrow, which made her quiver inside. Damn the man! Just when she was trying to forget him. What was he trying to do to her?

'Yes.' She tried to speak lightly. 'Fancy you remembering I saw all those.'

He gave a rueful smile. 'You should know I remember everything about you, Pippa.'

Of course. She reminded him of Olivia.

'I really have to go—'

'You've got plenty of time. I want to know more about this written paper. And I'm doing clinics this afternoon. There's no rush.'

At those words Pippa felt she was going to burst. Clinics! He was going to be in Outpatients! Oh, no—that would make it worse. How could she possibly avoid him?

Do you want to avoid him? asked a little voice inside her head. You want to torture yourself, don't you?

'Yes,' she whispered aloud. He leaned forward, watching her.

'Wasn't there a question on hyperemesis?' Why did he have to remind her of Olivia? Well, she wasn't going to be disconcerted. She smiled.

'Not this time. How is Olivia, by the way? I hear she's gone home.'

'Olivia's fine. It was psychological. Once the problem was resolved, she soon recovered.'

The problem was resolved. He'd gone back to her. Pippa fiddled with her watch strap, aware of his blue eyes on her.

'You disappeared from Six,' he remarked. 'Where have you been?'

'On Two and Three. And Outpatients from today.'

His eyes widened. 'This afternoon?'

Her throat was so tight she could hardly speak. 'Yes.'

'Shall we go back together?' She could hardly contain herself. This was sheer torture, but it was better than parting.

'Why not?'

He laid a hand on her shoulder as they left, and Pippa was aware of curious glances. His touch was like fire, burning her.

They walked silently along the corridor to Outpatients. There didn't seem to be any need for words. Pippa wanted the moment to last for ever, Julian at her side. As they reached the waiting area Sister came out of her office.

'Nurse Garland. I've put you in charge of case histories, all the new patients. Good afternoon, Dr Reed.'

Julian smiled and went on ahead. Pippa felt as though the bottom had fallen out of her world. Taking case histories meant she wouldn't see Julian at all. She went to fetch the pile of folders from reception. It was a big pile, it would keep her busy most of the afternoon. Ah well, perhaps it was for the best.

She called the name on the top folder, and a round-faced girl with long mousy hair got up. Pippa led her into an interview room, and placed the folder on the desk.

*　　　*　　　*

The afternoon passed quickly, and Pippa had only thought about Julian three times. At four o'clock she'd finished, and went along to see Sister.

'Finished? Right, perhaps you'd like to help round the back? There can't be many more to see.'

Pippa entered the first cubicle she saw that didn't have a nurse present. The patient was a West Indian girl on her first visit. She smiled when she saw Pippa.

'Hello, again,' said Pippa. 'Nervous?'

'You bet!'

'It's not too bad. And the doctors are all

very nice.'

'We are, aren't we?' came Julian's voice behind her. 'Hallo, Madeline. First baby and first visit, I see. Well, there's no need to be scared.'

Madeline smiled nervously. Julian put on his sterile gloves and began. He soon put the girl at her ease, and soon she was laughing and giggling. Pippa helped from the couch and tidied the trolley, making sure the syringes of blood were labelled correctly and placed in the rack for the laboratory.

One by one the patients left. Once the last one had gone so did the doctors, the junior housemen and students listening intently to the wise words of the consultants. As Julian passed Pippa, he didn't seem to be aware of her, as she bustled about, tidying cubicles, restocking trolleys. It was soon done, and she was alone for a moment. She'd watched Julian leave with the others, and it had felt as though a small part of her had gone with him. She went across to the window that ran the length of the room, and looked out at the traffic and people. She wondered what Australia would be like. A strange country, strange people. She wouldn't see Julian again.

She felt her heart was breaking. Her throat hurt, her eyes filled with tears. She'd thought she'd cried out all her tears that day when she'd come back without a car, and without a heart. Yet now they squeezed out against her will, and trickled down her cheeks. She didn't wipe them away, but surrendered to the luxury of her emotions. She heard soft footsteps, and she tensed. She brushed her cheek with her hands.

'You're crying,' came the voice she both longed and dreaded to hear.

'No, I'm not. Why should I be crying?' She swallowed hard.

'Then look at me.'

'I—I'm rather busy.' As she turned away from him he took her arm.

'It's all done.'

'No—it isn't—' She pulled away from him and went into the nearest cubicle. She moved the instruments on the trolley.

'Pippa.' He had followed her, but she refused to look at him. Her legs felt like jelly.

'Have I upset you, Pippa? Tell me.'

'I'm not upset! I'm busy.'

'Don't make excuses.' He sounded cross. Pippa clenched her fists. Why wouldn't he go away! 'I thought you liked me, Pippa. Why are you avoiding me?'

Because I love you, I love you, I love you!

'I like you. I have no reason to dislike you.' But I hate you for playing with my heart.

'You're not still upset over Neil?'

'Of course not.' Foolishly, she told the truth. She could have used that as a reason for crying.

'Perhaps there's—someone else?'

244

'No—no, there's no one else.'

'Then what has upset you? You can tell me. I'm your friend.'

His gentle understanding tone made her lose control. 'How can you be my friend, after what you did?'

She moved away from him, to the other side of the couch. This was where Madeline had lain, this was where Julian's hands had gently and expertly examined her, touched her in the most intimate places. Pippa squirmed inside. She had been in danger of imagining those hands touching her, in the same intimate places. Her face grew pink. She moved jerkily to straighten the sheet, and the long envelope fell from her pocket. She bent to pick it up but Julian was quicker. He read the address aloud.

'Give me that! It's private!'

His face had changed. 'Australia? You're going to work in Australia? What has made you do this?'

'I'm free to work where I like. Give me my letter!'

'What did you mean when you said, "after what I did"?'

'I shouldn't need to tell you.' She ran from the cubicle, down the long room, towards the empty waiting-room. She could hear his footsteps behind her. A girl with auburn hair, carrying a baby, was crossing the entrance to the waiting room. She glanced at Pippa, and stopped.

'Hallo! Nurse Garland, isn't it? Don't you remember me? Diane Emery?'

'Of course I remember you. How are you?' Julian had stopped behind her, and placed his hand on her shoulder. He still held the letter.

'I'm fine,' said Diane. 'And I have you to thank for it. And this is Dr Reed, isn't it? I really should have come to thank you for saving Simon and me.'

'All part of the job,' said Julian. 'You were very lucky.'

'I know. I took Simon home last week. I just brought him for a check up. He's five and a half pounds now.' She glanced from Pippa to Julian. 'You make a handsome couple, you know,' she laughed cheekily, and hurried away.

Immediately, Pippa moved away from Julian, saying, 'My letter, please.'

'But you're not going to Australia. I shan't let you.'

'Oh? And how will you stop me?'

'I shall marry you, that's what I shall do.'

For a long moment the world seemed to stand still. She couldn't believe he could be so cruel.

'How can you say such a thing?' she whispered, blinking back the tears. 'Why do you have to torture me so?'

He moved quickly to her, and lifted her chin with his fingers.

'Torture you? When I tell you the truth? That I love you? That I've always loved you,

246

from the moment you trod on my toes—'

'I didn't!'

'—nearly trod on my toes.'

'How can you say you love me when you're going to marry Olivia?'

'Olivia? I thought I explained about—'

'It was all lies, wasn't it, Julian? I saw you, you held her in your arms, and she said you'd made her very happy, and she wanted you to tell her all over again. I heard it all!'

'Oh, Pippa, Pippa, you silly, silly little fool! I'd just brought her a message from Felix, he'd rung me to tell me about a house he'd been negotiating to buy for her, a house she'd always wanted, but it belonged to Lisa Carlton. I'd gone straight to tell her.'

'Lisa Carlton? Her house? But she did tell me she was in love with you.'

'She's in love with everyone, is Olivia. I told you what she was like. Why didn't you believe me? Didn't you trust me?'

'I suppose I was jumping to conclusions,' she whispered, as he drew her into his arms. She looked into his blue eyes and felt she was drowning. His lips touched hers lightly, like a feather.

'Did I hear you say you love me?' she whispered.

'I've always loved you, from the first day I saw you.'

'And all the time I thought you disliked me, because I look like Olivia. You'd never talk about her—'

'Because she was part of my life I preferred to forget. I'd been so infatuated with her, and then she'd jilted me. It was a terrible blow to my ego. I wanted you so much, Pippa, but you had Neil—'

'I think he's got Lucy now. She's going to Chile with him next year.'

'And you're going to Australia. I shall have to come with you.'

'But I didn't really want to go. I just couldn't stand seeing you, knowing you could never be mine.'

She rested her head on his chest. Their hearts seemed to beat in unison.

'Does that mean you're in love with me?' His voice was husky.

'Since the first time I saw you, when I trod—' They both laughed merrily. Julian's blue eyes were still searching her face, as if he were looking for the love she'd declared.

'I have to tell you something,' said Pippa, safe and secure in his arms.

'Ah—confession time.'

'When I heard the new registrar had turned up at Mike Badger's leaving party, I didn't know it was you, and I imagined you were bald and fat with warts on your nose.'

Julian roared with laughter. 'Warts? Bald? Mr Reed, the new consultant?'

'Consultant? Oh, that's marvellous, Julian! It's absolutely marvellous.'

'Would you rather I were bald and fat with warts on my nose, Pippa?' he asked teasingly. 'I suppose, when we're old—and, of course, you might have warts by then.' He gently traced the shape of her mouth with his finger.

'Oh, Julian, I don't care what you look like when we're old. I shall always love you just as you are.'

His deep blue eyes fixed hungrily on hers.

'And I love every red hair of your head,' he murmured, holding her so tight she could hardly breathe.

He placed his lips on hers, and she clung to him, her hands stroking his neck and face. There was no sound, except for wildly beating hearts, and the rushing in Pippa's head as she responded to his wild, passionate kiss.

The letter to Australia fell to the floor. No one noticed. And no one cared.

Chivers Large Print Direct

If you have enjoyed this Large Print book and would like to build up your own collection of Large Print books and have them delivered direct to your door, please contact **Chivers Large Print Direct**.

Chivers Large Print Direct offers you a full service:

⬦ **Created to support your local library**

⬦ **Delivery direct to your door**

⬦ **Easy-to-read type and attractively bound**

⬦ **The very best authors**

⬦ **Special low prices**

For further details either call Customer Services on 01225 443400 or write to us at

Chivers Large Print Direct
FREEPOST (BA 1686/1)
Bath
BA1 3QZ